MW01045665

Stories of the Old Testament

Jacob Klein

DENVER, COLORADO

Stories of the Old Testament
All Rights Reserved.
Copyright © 2016 Jacob Klein
v1.0

Outskirts Press, Inc.
http://www.outskirtspress.com

ISBN: 978-1-4787-4884-7

Outskirts Press and the "OP" logo are trademarks belonging to Outskirts Press, Inc.

PRINTED IN THE UNITED STATES OF AMERICA

Introduction

I have always enjoyed stories of the Bible, be it the story of the creation, the exodus of the Israelites from bondage in Egypt, or the great stories of kings like David and Solomon. You also have Noah's flood, the passing of judgment on Sodom and Gomorrah, the building of the tower of Babel, and God's response to that, as well as great women in the stories, like Ruth, Esther, and one of the judges named Deborah. You have people rising to great heights like Gideon, who led Israel to many great victories, in spite of his lack of confidence, as well as those who were brought down to new depths, such as Saul for his arrogant attitude in thinking that his ways were better than the Lord's. You also have those who, once they did fall, still found a way to redeem themselves in the end, such as Samson, who lost his strength and his way when he fell into lust with Delilah, a person who was a Philistine, the very people Samson tried to fight against, but in his final act atoned for his mistakes.

In the New Testament, you have all the stories and miracles of Jesus, as well as the fact that Jesus was so willing to save humanity from their mistakes that He was willing to die in the most humiliating and barbaric way possible, being hung on a cross like a scummy criminal, only to rise from the grave on the third day. Later on, His apostles, and then Paul, would continue on His mission and message of hope, love, and the true meaning of leading through serving. Of course, I will only talk about stories from the Old Testament in this particular book, but the New Testament is no less interesting.

The reason why I am writing about stories that have already been written thousands of years ago is that people can become confused about certain passages, as well as the fact that some books in the Bible fail to capture people's imagination. The book of Leviticus, for instance, has all sorts of rules and regulations so that if you read them for more than a couple of minutes, you would fall asleep really fast, and many (but not all) of these rules have already been compensated for once Jesus died on the cross. There is no more need for animal sacrifices because Jesus became the ultimate sacrifice for our sins. There are some rules, however, that must be followed even to this day, since once we receive God's forgiveness, we must do all we can to change our conduct and hearts for the better. For instance, it would be wise to obey what the Bible teaches about homosexuality, a topic that will be covered briefly in my writings.

In the end, though, all I have to say is that as much as I would like for people to read what I write (and believe me, I really do), it is also much more crucial for people to read the Bible for themselves. Do not base any conclusions of what the Bible says or means just because Jacob Klein, Billy Graham, or anyone else says you should believe what they say, but rather draw your own conclusions based on how you interpret a certain passage, for God loves someone who not only does His will but is someone who is educated enough to think for themselves. Now, that is not to say that you shouldn't ask for guidance from a parent, a friend, or a local minister, but in the end, you should still have the freedom to make up your own mind, based on reading of scripture, as well as that all-important way to communicate, through praying to the Father above, who made all things possible. So I hope you enjoy this book, but more important, I hope that you will have a better understanding of the greatest book of all time, the Bible.

Chapter 1
Human Fall (Genesis, chs.1–3)*

"Let's get some fig leaves, so that we may cover our nakedness," Adam told Eve.

Yes, Adam and Eve were in serious trouble, as both realized that they were naked and were, therefore, ashamed of it. Yet the irony was that neither Adam nor Eve even thought about their own nudity when they first appeared. In fact, the reason why for their initial lack of awareness was because they were the only two human beings to have been made by God, instead of being born inside a mother's womb like every other human being has been ever since, and also, let's face it, even if they did realize it, nobody else like them was even around. However, as we will see, Adam and Eve did something to disobey their Creator, something, in fact, that was so horrendous that they felt shame over their nudity that they hadn't experienced before, and now they were going to be punished for their actions, and that punishment would change the course of human history.

Before we go any further with this story of Adam and Eve, let us start at the very beginning. Literally. In Genesis 1:1–2, it is mentioned that not only did God

1

create the heavens and the earth but also that when these things were created, there was nothing there. That's right, just a big void in the universe. Except that the only thing that was around was the spirit of God. This is crucial, for it points out God's divinity. After all, if He were not totally divine, there is no way He would not have been born, made, or created in some sort of fashion, but as it is, He was always there, still is here, and will always be around.

The first thing that God created, of course, was light, and when I say light, I do not mean that God turned on a switch, or invented a flashlight, or lit a match and put it in a lantern. No, all God did was use the spoken word. "Let there be light," (Genesis 1:3) He said, and thus, light appeared in the vast darkness of the universe. For the first day, God's work was complete, but there was to be more.

Now, before I go on to what happens on the second day, I'd like to point out the significance of God creating light in the middle of the vast darkness. First, the fact that God only needed the spoken word is, in fact, significant. Think of the times we do pray. In essence, what we are doing is communicating to our Creator. We are talking with Him, and hopefully, we are also listening to Him in our hearts. Now, look up Matthew 7:7–8. This was where Jesus was telling the crowds some parables. If you notice in just those two verses, Jesus was revealing a key principle in God's kingdom. All one has to do is ask God, seek God, and knock on His door. Basically, be persistent, not just in asking for God's favor but also in living your life according to God's standards. So, when one looks at it, when we ask and communicate with God, we are using a spoken word of faith that breaks down limits.

Another thing to consider is that light was God's first creation. Without light, how could we know what exists, or what could be in front of us? For instance, what if I told you to stand in the darkest area possible, a place where no light is shining? Now, what if I told you that I was holding a baseball? Would you believe me? Perhaps, but since I am a mere man communicating to you, I could be lying. I might not be honest about the object that I am holding up. In fact, I might not be holding up an object at all! In any event, what I am saying is that God created light not just to give life to the world we live in today but also to reveal truth.

Finally, there is the factor of light being the only thing God creates on the very first day. Why is that? Is it because God is limited in His abilities? Absolutely not! However, in this story, God was revealing yet another one of His principles, and that is to trust not in what He will do but the timing of His will.

The next two days of God's creation would give our planet more depth. You have skies, waters, and the ground and dirt itself that start to take shape. As great as light is, if God stopped there, it would have been such an eyesore and would lack depth. It would be like me holding a flashlight with the bulb on about a half an inch from your eyeballs. After a while, all you would want is for the darkness to return. However, by adding skies, water, and land, now you have more depth, and a better picture. Now, you see that God did not make light just for the sake of making light. He revealed that there was a purpose behind it. Throw in plants and vegetation as well, and now you know that His purpose behind all of this was to create life.

Plant life by itself, though, could be dangerous, because what they need is time and seasons to grow. Now, where I live, in Western New York, we have virtually zero vegetation during the winter months, other than some trees. The reason for this is obvious: snow covers the plants, so all they are getting is moisture, which is great because you do not want plants to dry up, but they cannot get nutrients because the snow blocks them from sunlight. So God now gave the earth some order in the form of sun, moon, and stars. Sun gives plants the nutrients; the moon is important for tides and ocean currents so that plants do not dry up or drown from lack of sunlight, and the stars provide a little bit of extra light during the nighttime. More important, though, is that God also dictated when these features appeared, so as to determine seasons.

Now, after four days of God's Creation, we had light, earth, skies, seas; we had plant life, as well, and we had sun, moon, and stars, as well as the timing of these things to determine seasons. Now was the time for God to create animals of every kind. Fish and whales for the seas, birds that could fly in the air, and land animals like lions, elephants, horses, giraffes, and other creatures as well. Some, like frogs and alligators, could travel either on land or the sea. And since the plants were already made, many of these creatures could sustain themselves by eating these things. Some, like tigers, had to eat some of the other animals, but the point is the same, that animals were to be provided as well.

All of this was great, but there was one thing lacking, and that was an authority figure on earth. This was where God's creation of man comes in. God did this wonderful thing, and he made man in His image. This man was designed to now have one task, and that task was to have dominion over plants and animals. What this entailed was that this man had such authority that he could even name all the animals. God had given this creature such responsibility that He now had an earthly counterpart to bring order to these animals and plants.

What I find fascinating is how God created man. You see, everybody who lives today is born out of a mother's womb, and we'll get to that later on. However, God formed the first man, not out of a womb, per se, but rather from the ground, the very dirt itself that God made before. The best way to describe this is if someone makes a clay pot; only in this instance, you are not making a utensil or cup, but rather forming a living, human being, and you are breathing air into it. In fact, there is a reference in Jeremiah 18:6 where God stated that He could do to the people of Israel just as a potter forms the shape of clay.

Now, where was this garden that this man, whom God named Adam, was supposed to tend? It was in a place called the Garden of Eden. In fact, this garden was so beautiful and filled with life that no man has ever created one that could be its equal. Also, the location of the place had to be precise. There had to have been a great river for this garden that flowed downstream, and this river had to have flowed into four more rivers after that. These four rivers were known as the Euphrates, Tigris, Pishon, and Gihon Rivers, respectively. Everyone who knows geography knows where the Tigris and Euphrates rivers are, since they reside around modern-day Iraq, but the Pishon and Gihon Rivers are a little more difficult to know, since these rivers either dried up or had their names changed to something else. The possibility, however, was that they could also have resided somewhere in the Persian Gulf region, since it would make sense if the narrative of this story was correct, that a river existed that flowed to four other rivers.

In any event, you still had this magnificent garden, the Garden of Eden, and it had all sorts of lush vegetation. There were two trees, however, that stood out among all of the vegetation. First, there was the Tree of Life, and the reason why this tree was named as such was obvious: it had

6

the fruit necessary to provide eternal life to anyone who eats it. The second tree, though, was different, because the second tree was known as the Tree of Knowledge, knowing good and evil. This tree was the one that God commanded Adam not to eat, for if he ate the fruit from this particular tree, he would surely die. The significance of the Tree of Knowledge was to be revealed later on.

Now, I bet you are wondering when Adam had a woman to keep him company. After all, you cannot have humanity exist today if you do not have both men and women around, and we'll get to that soon. First, though, there is a character who should be mentioned that would be significant in the story of the Garden of Eden, and why this chapter is entitled "Human Fall." If you look up Isaiah 14:12, you will notice that God made an angel, and this angel was named Lucifer, and Lucifer was the most beautiful angel God ever created. However, there was one problem: Lucifer at some point looked over his own beauty, and instead of praising God for it, he developed a narcissism about himself and started to think that he could run heaven better than God Himself.

Now, keep in mind that God created other angels as well, and only good exist in heaven. There is no evil in heaven, and because of that, there was nothing to tempt Lucifer, or the other angels, into doing what was wrong. With these factors involved, why would Lucifer not only disobey God and believe in his own hype but lead an armed rebellion by convincing some of the other angels into war against their Creator? The reason for this is that God does want His creation to have something called confidence. You see, confidence in and of itself is not a bad quality at all. With confidence, someone can push through even the most difficult of circumstances. The problem, though, in having confidence is that if it is not directed into having confidence in God but solely on one's own self, then it becomes a trait known as pride, and it was the mistake Lucifer, aka Satan, made, is that he was so egotistical that he believed that he could run heaven better than God and destroy his own Creator as well. Not surprisingly, God defeated Satan and banished him from His kingdom, but God did not destroy Satan entirely, and the reason for this is because God wanted us to serve Him out of love, as opposed to obligation. This part of the story, of course, would end up being very significant in the events that happen not too long afterwards.

Now, on to the story of how a woman, also known as Eve, was made. Adam was happy that God had given him dominion over all the Earth, and the responsibility of naming plants, fruits, and animals of every kind. This was something to behold, that a man could name animals, such as tigers, elephants, bears, turtles, frogs, et cetera. However, Adam was not pleased on two fronts. First, as the only human being on the planet, Adam did not have any help whatsoever in maintaining this dominion that he had, and since he was not God, he couldn't be everywhere at once. The second reason why Adam was not completely satisfied is that he kept noticing that all the animals that he was tending to were male and female, and furthermore, they also were commissioned by God earlier to go forth and multiply. This disturbed Adam, since he longed to have find some sort of companionship that actually involved someone of the same species.

Well, if Adam wanted a female in his life, God was going to provide a way that would be possible. So what God does was He put Adam in a deep sleep. So deep, in fact, that Adam was not aware at the time of what God did next. For what God did next was He took one of Adam's ribs out of his body, and out of this one rib, God created a female companion that Adam had so long desired to have. Personally, I could see why Adam had to be put into a deep sleep for this; it would be very discomforting to watch someone or something be formed out of one of your ribs, and it would be downright painful to have one of your bones be literally ripped out of your body.

At the end of the second chapter of Genesis, it made mention of a man having to leave his parents behind, in order to meet with a woman, and once that happened, the two became one flesh. In his movie *Unstoppable*, Kirk Cameron made mention of Adam being one person, and God created a second individual, this time a woman, but when Adam woke up, the first thing he said was "This is bone of my bone, and flesh of my flesh." Basically, one man was used to create a second being, but when they were united, they became one flesh. This was the basic premise of how and for what purpose this female, who we all know was Eve, was made, but it went further than that.

For instance, the fact that Adam was made from the dust of the Earth but Eve was made from one of Adam's ribs showed that God was flexible enough to attain similar results but use different methods. This was important because if God did things the same way over and over again, people would be able to expect what happens next, and there would be no reason to have that agent we call faith.

Another thing to consider is the fact that Adam and Eve were, in fact, of "one flesh." The meaning of this is significant. Everyone knows about how in every Judeo-Christian wedding, the priest or pastor, or whoever is the leader of a church, makes mention of this story. However, what most people do not understand is that what God was saying here was that he wanted each man to live his own life, marry, and start a new family of his own, instead of always residing with his parents. That being said, we must also remember that we <u>should do this on God's own timing, not our own</u>. So, before you teenagers just go ahead and start a family without your parents' consent, remember that you should do so not only because God says it is time but because that the person you are with is the one God Himself has ordained to spend time with you for the rest of your life.

Then, there is the matter in Genesis 2:25; it was mentioned that Adam and Eve were, hold for it, naked, but they did not feel ashamed of it at the time. The reason for this is evident: sin had not entered into their hearts just yet; therefore, they could not be condemned for their lack of dress. As long as they did not eat from the Tree of Knowledge, knowing good and evil, they were safe. They could walk around in the nude as long as they wanted to, yet not feel any guilt over it. Of course, as we all know, events would take a turn for the worse, and the situation would change with it.

Remember that guy named Lucifer, aka Satan, aka the Devil? Yeah, the one who started a failed rebellion against God? The one some people still foolishly believe is easy to spot, believing that he has horns on his head and a tail and carries a trident? Well, it just so happened that he was there in the garden, but he was disguised as a serpent. And wouldn't you know it, he just so happened to be on the very tree that Adam and Eve were commanded by God not to eat from. The reasoning why Satan was there was pretty obvious: Satan figured that the best way to counteract God was to have God's most prized creation, man, turn their backs on Him. Not only because Satan knew full well that he could never defeat God by himself but also because the fact that man serving Satan would break

God's heart. Also, Satan hated man to begin with, since man had dominion over all the Earth, and Satan wanted to have that position all by himself, so if the human race was destroyed, that would be okay in the Devil's book, since it would open up for him to take over the planet.

Satan started with Eve. He first got her attention by calling out her name. Then, once he got her attention, Satan asked Eve if there were any tree that God had commanded her and Adam not to eat from. She responded by stating that any fruit from any tree could be eaten, except for this particular tree that she was standing under. Satan told her that no, the fruit from this Tree of Knowledge, knowing good and evil, would not kill her or Adam. In fact, Satan stated that it would give them knowledge like God, knowing the difference between good and evil, which was something that their Creator did not want them to have. Besides, just look at how luscious and wonderful this fruit looked. Come on, Eve, surely such fruit could not be bad for you.

Surely, Eve would say no to this, right? After all, she had been told repeatedly by both God and Adam that she should not eat fruit from this particular tree, and it was only just now that something else told her otherwise. There was no way that Eve would fall for such a trap, right? Surely, Eve would just say no to this, kind of like a drug commercial in the 1980s, right?

Wrong! Eve went right ahead and ate the fruit from

the Tree of Knowledge. She fell for this trick, especially with how good the fruit looked on it, but also, the fact that she could acquire God-like knowledge was very appealing, indeed. At first, it seemed like this new creature was right. Eve did not die, at least not yet, from eating out of this tree; in fact, she did acquire some knowledge. It obviously did not help Eve's cause that Adam was not doing his duties as a husband should and not watching out and protecting her in all circumstances. This was clearly Satan's strategy, and has been ever since, to go after a weak link, someone who does not have any backup support and relies solely on himself or herself instead of relying on God, because such a person, alone, can never stand up to the adversities and temptations that the Devil throws.

So, when Adam came back, and Eve told him that she already had eaten from the Tree of Knowledge, and that it was okay to eat, that eating from such a tree would give him knowledge, Adam took a bite out of this fruit himself, and it is understandable why. God had told them that such fruit from this tree would kill them, and yet, it appears that it does not do so, because here was a person who did eat this fruit, and yet she was not dead; in fact, she seemed to have acquired knowledge that she didn't have before. So Adam ate from the forbidden fruit, and yet, once this new knowledge took hold in their minds, they realized that something is amiss. They figured out that they were naked, and Adam and Eve started to feel this shame of their nudity, something they had not experienced before, and once this happened, they realized that they were in big trouble with their Creator, and He was not going to take their actions too kindly.

Before we go any further, some of you might ask yourselves a couple of questions. For instance, why would God, if he loved His creation so much, allow both Adam and Eve to be tempted to eat such a fruit, and then to actually let them do it? Also, why would God allow such a rebellious angel like Satan to live so that he could tempt mankind into doing evil? The reason for this is because God gives both angels and man the freedom to choose, and it is this ability to choose that allows for sincere worship of God, instead of one that is produced by fear. Now, in this manner of choice, Satan made a choice to rebel against God, and Adam and Eve made the choice to eat the forbidden fruit, but the fact remains that such actions have consequences, and in this case, those consequences were not pleasant.

Well, God was walking through the Garden of Eden, although in reality God is everywhere at once, asking Adam where he was. Truthfully, being everywhere at once, God knew what both Adam and Eve had done, that both of them had eaten the forbidden fruit. What God was looking for is their response, to see if they were truly sorry for their actions. So, as soon as God called for Adam, Adam responded by telling God that he was afraid to reveal himself and tried to cover his nakedness. Wait a minute, though! God never told Adam and Eve that they were naked, and the only way to have known about this was if somebody, or more specifically, somebodies, had eaten out of the Tree of Knowledge. God, needless to say, got right to the point, and asked Adam if he had eaten out of this forbidden tree, and this was Adam's chance at redemption. All it would have taken was for Adam to say something along the lines of "I am sorry, God. I didn't mean to eat out of this tree, but now I am asking for your forgiveness, and I promise never to do it again". At least it would have allowed him to stay in the garden.

So, what did Adam, this supposedly noble husband, do? He blamed Eve for it! Adam stated that he would not have eaten from such a tree, except that Eve made him do it. In essence, instead of forgiveness, Adam tried to rationalize his actions, which was no way to earn God's favor. However, God did ask Eve about her actions, to give her the same opportunity He gave Adam to ask for forgiveness, and just like Adam, she blamed someone else, or in this case, she blamed the serpent in the garden for talking her into it.

Now was the time for God to bring down His judgment. The serpent was now condemned to crawl upon the Earth, and there was to be continual war between the descendants of the serpent and the descendants of Eve. Eventually, a man would come out and destroy all evil, which happened when Jesus Christ Himself conquered death by rising from the grave.

Eve, for listening to a talking serpent and giving in to its temptation, would not only have great labor pains in childbirth but also would have to be submissive to Adam's will. Although the last forty-plus years have produced great strides in women's rights, the fact remains that some cultures still treat women as nothing more than property, and Eve's actions are the reason why. As for childbearing, the same formula still holds true today. The first few months are not too bad, and the woman is excited over new life being created. After a while, though, the woman starts to get a little cranky and tired, due to the pressure of a growing fetus inside her body. By the time the child is about to be born, everybody better steer clear, because things will get ugly.

If you think Adam got away without any sort of repercussions, though, think again. Adam now had to grow his own food, instead of it being provided in the Garden of Eden. This involved toilsome labor, the type of labor that Adam would now be feeling after a while. His hands would be sore from the thistles and thorns, and his back would be killing him from bending over for planting and harvesting. Lastly, both man and woman were to be banished from the Garden of Eden, in order that they did not eat from the Tree of Life, since they had to pay for disobeying God somehow, and because of this banishment, men and women have tasted death since.

After this banishment, Adam and Eve would go on to have children, but in Genesis 4, Cain and Abel would have the first war, with Cain slaying Abel because Abel offered a more pleasing sacrifice to God. Ever since then, man has continued to sin and die, and it is only through God's grace that there is even an opportunity for repentance. <u>All this because man made the wrong choice and listened to the promise of a talking serpent, as hard as it is to believe, instead of the Holy of Holies.</u>

*While not necessarily quoting word for word, each chapter of this book will have at least one chapter of the Bible that it is referring to. Every single one of these, I am referring to the New International Version Study Bible, 10th Anniversary edition, copyright 1995. The same source is also used if I have a Bible verse in parentheses during the course of a chapter, as well as if I add a plus sign and note to it. For example, if you see (Exodus 1:8+note), that means that both the verse and the note that corresponds with it came from the New International Version Study Bible, 10th Anniversary edition.

Chapter 2
Floody, Floody
(Genesis 4–9)

Initially, it was a great and wonderful sign of relief. After over a century of drought, the rains finally came. Now, it appeared, the crops would finally get the water needed in order to survive. Little did these people know, however, that not one of them would be alive 40 days later, other than the man they ridiculed all that time for building a boat on dry land, along with his wife, his three sons, and the three women who married them.

To begin this story, let's go back to when Cain slayed Abel. Obviously, this event happened because Cain was jealous of God showing favor to his brother Abel and his sacrifice but not doing so over the sacrifice made by Cain. Cain first tried to hide what he had done and later on ran away. Why? Because God knew what Cain had done, that he murdered his brother, and that spirit of condemnation was so strong that Cain feared for his life. Considering that the only people living on Earth at the time were his parents, Adam and Eve, and maybe any sisters he might have had, this seemed far-fetched, to say the least.

Whatever the case, God puts a mark on Cain's head, as a reminder that vengeance would be taken seven-fold on anyone who killed him. Personally, I think the mark on Cain's head was a symbol of the Tree of Knowledge, and He used it as a reminder that even though this man Cain was a murderer, the fact remains that you are no better than he is because of the sin Adam and Eve made in the Garden of Eden.

Anyway, Cain did eventually marry and have some kids. In other words, he married one of his sisters, but before anyone judges this as immoral, remember that the only people on Earth at the time were Cain's parents and any siblings he might have had. They had to populate the Earth somehow, and since nobody else even existed, well, they had to make love with their kin. In today's world, though, such behavior is inexcusable. There are well over six billion people on our planet today; you should be able to find someone outside your family!

Meanwhile, Adam and Eve were devastated because not only was Abel dead but their other son Cain was now AWOL, so they need some sort of good news, and they eventually did get it in the birth of their third son, Seth. He, of course, like Cain, would marry and have descendants, as well. Thus, generation by generation, the Earth was getting to be more and more populated by mankind.

Unfortunately, since man now knew that he had a choice of doing good or evil, their inclination was towards doing what was wrong. Another murder occurred, when Lamech, one of Cain's descendants, murdered another man for wounding him. He did end up with three very gifted sons: Jabal, who was known for his sheepherding and building tents; Jubal, for his ability to play music; and Tubal-Cain, who could forge all sorts of metals, such as iron and bronze. However, what these men, and others, lack, was an appreciation for the One who created all.

One thing that was interesting was what was mentioned at the beginning of Genesis 6, and the reason why it is fascinating is because it mentioned some of the sons of God marrying the daughters of men. What could this mean? Some say that it was merely descendants of Cain marrying the descendants of Seth, while others would argue that it was really fallen angels of God who disobeyed Him at some point that were doing this. In fact, the word "Nephilim" is a Hebrew word meaning "fallen ones" (Genesis 6:4+note). In either case, what you now had were men from such offspring who were held in special admiration in the eyes of man, but what God was seeing was deplorable and an abomination in His eyes.

It is sad to say that in this time period, only two men were not corrupted in their own hearts. The first was a man named Enoch, who was the seventh generation of Seth's descendants, but he had a very rare instance where he did not face death but was taken up to heaven. Later on, another righteous man appears on the scene, by the name of Noah, and God was to ask Noah for a great task, something that he, as the only man who was guided by God's will and asked for His direction in life, could possibly understand.

By the time God had asked Noah for this specific task, the whole world was corrupt, to the point where God was grieving over the fact that He had even bothered to create man in the first place, since their evil and sin were so great. So now was the time for God to make a clean sweep over all the Earth. Oh yes, it will receive rain, all right! It will receive so much rain that nothing on Earth was safe. Men, women, children, animals, trees, and crops would all feel the Almighty's wrath and be flooded out. Only Noah and his family would be safe from the destruction to come, and that was on the condition that they obeyed God's command.

Here was Noah's role. Noah was to make an ark, or boat, out of cypress wood, and cover it with some pitch, inside and out. The size of the ark was to be 300 cubits long, 50 cubits in width, and 30 cubits high. A cubit is equivalent to 1 1/2 feet, so you are talking about 450 feet in length, 75 feet in width, and 45 feet in height (Genesis 6:15+note). A roof was to be placed on top of it, no higher than 1 cubit, or 18 inches, and there were to be lower, middle, and upper decks. Most important, though, Noah was to not only saved himself and his family in this boat but also bring two of every kind of animal into it, as well, one of each gender.

So Noah went to work and started to build the ark. He continued to do so for the next 100 years of his life, day and night. Even when everyone else was ridiculing him for being a fool and building a boat on dry land, Noah continued his task. This is a credit to the persistent faith and work ethic that Noah possessed; it would have been very easy for Noah to give up and think to himself that maybe he was a fool and that it wasn't really God calling him to build a boat, but build it he did, right down to the very last detail on God's own blueprint. Plus, since Noah believed it was God giving him a warning that He was about to flood the Earth, Noah knew enough that he had to obey this command.

The next step would be a monumental challenge in its own right, and that was to bring the animals into the ark without tearing each other apart. Many believe that with the dimensions of the ark being what they were, that it would have been an impossibility for the ark to fit all the animals inside of it. However, there are some things to consider here. For one thing, there is no way that sea creatures would be put inside the ark, and there would be no need to, since the Earth was being flooded anyway; they would have all the water they would ever need to swim in. Another thing to consider is that while it was mentioned that the animals had to be brought in two by two, it did not mean that they had to be a specific species.

For instance, a male and a female tiger would have to be brought in, but it did not mean that you necessarily had to bring in a pair of Bengal tigers first, then another pair, but this one being Siberian tigers. Then you had some of the other animals, like sheep and doves, that had to be used for a sacrifice unto the Lord, which were actually seven of every kind, and you would then realize that there was just enough room to fit all the animals in that needed to be in.

Once the preparations were made, the floods came, and they came in the 600th year of Noah's life. I am sure that those who were not part of Noah's family were relieved at first; their vegetation would finally have a chance to grow and not be scorched by the sun. However, it soon became apparent that not only did this flood mean business but also it was not to be designed to merely help crops grow. Those who had mocked and ridiculed Noah before were now scrambling towards the ark in hopes of possibly saving their lives. There was one problem, though; they could not get inside. The doors were all sealed shut, and it was locked so that those outside could not get in, and those inside were not to get out. Basically, it had more security and was locked better than a computer with the most advanced technology designed for the prevention of identity theft. Even the highest of mountains were engulfed by this flood, and by a significant margin, I might add.

What is amazing in all of this was that while people on

the outside of the ark were getting destroyed by the flood, the ark itself was just floating along on the waters without any trouble. Remember God's instructions to Noah as to how to construct the ark in the first place? Well, God had given Noah these instructions because that was to be the precise design of the boat that could withstand the flood that God had intended to bring in order to wipe out mankind. However, even with the right dimensions, as well as wood as strong as cypress wood, Noah still had to cover the wood with pitch. There was a reason for this. Wood has a tendency to expand or contract based on how water hits it. This is important because once this happens, the structure of the wood becomes weakened. However, by putting pitch on the wood, Noah unknowingly was giving the wood the sturdiness it needed to withstand the pounding of the waves of water that were hitting against the ark.

Of course, eventually the waters would recede once everyone and everything outside the ark was destroyed, until the ark landed on the mountains of Ararat. It was here that Noah opened up one of the windows to the ark, so that he could find out if it was safe to get out of it. First, he sent a raven to search for land. I guess that the raven had other plans, though, and he never stopped flying all over the place until the waters did recede, and truthfully, I don't blame the raven because you would want to enjoy that freedom that Noah had given you if you were stuck in a boat for 40 straight days.

So Noah then sent out a dove, and this dove proved to be very loyal to Noah. When it did not find land at first, it did return, mainly to regain its strength, but the dove returned nevertheless. Noah gave the bird seven days to recover and then sent the dove out again. This time, not only did the dove return but he also brought a freshly plucked olive branch with it. This was significant because olive branches come from fairly low places, and not on mountains; thus, it signaled that it was safe for Noah and his family to come out of the ark and settle on dry land.

God did make a covenant with Noah and with mankind afterwards, and the sign of this covenant came in the form of a rainbow. In other words, God was saying that He was resting His bow and would never again destroy the Earth again with a flood. Of course, this did not mean that man has stopped sinning ever since, but it did mean that if we come to God with a repentant heart and ask for forgiveness, though, that He is just and will show us His mercy, in addition to punishing the guilty.

There have been many other accounts of a "Great Flood" in the history of the world that bears some resemblance to Noah's account, the most famous being the Epic of Gilgamesh from the Old Babylonia Empire. Indeed, there are some materials that would be worth searching in Gilgamesh's account of a great flood, such as the specific name of the pitch used in the life-saving boat being a substance called bitumen. However, I am not a huge fan of Gilgamesh, and the reason for that is the differences between his account and Noah's. Gilgamesh, for instance, said that the boat was a cube square of 200X200X200 cubits, whereas Noah stated that his ark was 300 cubits long by 50 in width and 30 in height. Also, Noah's ark had three stories, whereas Gilgamesh stated that the boat was 6 stories high. Then you have Noah mentioning relatives and animals, while Gilgamesh only mentioned those of kin. All of this is found in the 1956 book <u>The Bible as History</u>, among other references.

There is one last thing to consider, though. Noah lived another 350 years after the flood happened; thus, he was 950 when he finally died. When you look at the next few generations, however, their ages decreased to where they struggle to make it past 200, and if you push it further than that, now you're talking about it being virtually impossible for mankind to live past 120. What this tells me is that the people in Noah's day must have had some of the best crops and eating habits man has ever known. Yet, in the end, these crops would be destroyed by the flood. Once the waters had receded, though, the plants and vegetation on Earth lost a lot of their previous vitality, and the reason for this was that the soil was not as good. In other words, people talk about living longer lives, and they can with the modern technology and know-how we have today, but there is still a limit as to how long you will live, and that limit is much shorter today than it was in Noah's day because mankind would not stop sinning. It just shows you that actions do indeed have serious consequences.

Chapter 3
They Asked for It
(Genesis 12–22)

This next story is similar to the one about Noah's flood in that if the people had turned their hearts to the Lord, then the tragedy that befell them could have been prevented. Unlike the flood, however, this destruction did not happen to the entire human race, but rather was confined to two pagan cities who did as they pleased, instead of doing all they could to please God.

To begin this story, we must first turn to Genesis 12 and 13. There was a man by the name of Abram who was commanded by God to have both him and his family leave the city of Ur and settle in the land of Canaan. Among those leaving Ur with Abram were Sarai, his wife, along with his nephew Lot. Eventually, Abram became a wealthy landowner because of how he made deals and concessions with the Egyptians, as well as his ability to maintain the land in pristine shape. The only problem was that since Lot had brought flocks and herds himself, and was rich in his own right, the land could not sustain both parties. Thus, there was a quarrel going on between

Abram's herdsmen and the herdsmen of Lot. Somehow, there had to be peace or else both parties would lose out.

If there was an example of the character and type of man that Abram was, it was revealed during this time. Abram could have told Lot to buzz off and mind his own business, and many would have thought that Abram would have been in the right to do so. After all, it was Abram that God called to settle in the land of Canaan, not Lot. However, even though Abram was in the right, it was more important for him to maintain peace in his family than to argue as to who should have possession of the land. So, as a man of peace, Abram decided to let Lot have whatever land Lot wanted.

Like most people, Lot chose the path of least resistance, which in this case was to go to the place where it would be easiest to grow your crops, and this area was in the plains near the Jordan River. Although peace was maintained inside the family for the time being, I am also sure that Abram must have felt that he got the short end of the stick. For on paper, it looked like Abram now owned nothing but desert and wasteland; only hardship and misery seemed to be in Abram's future. God, however, blessed Abram by telling him that he was to be the father of descendants as numerous as every grain of sand that was on the land that Abram owned at the time. This, even though Abram's land seemed like a perpetual wasteland and his wife Sarai was barren and could not produce an heir. As events would turn out, it was this image that God displayed that would be crucial in Abram's life, and his outlook, as well.

Meanwhile, Lot was having difficulties himself, and the worst part was that he had nothing to do with them. Yes, Lot did need Abram's help, and it was for a very good reason. There was a king by the name of Kedorlaomer (why they couldn't just name the guy John is beyond me!) who was starting to experience rebellion from some of his subjects, particularly those from Sodom and Gomorrah. Well, this did not settle too well with Kedorlaomer, who like most kings was willing to put down anybody considered a threat to his kingdom, so he called upon three other kings whom he considered to be his allies, in order to put down this rebellion. Not only did these kings crush the uprising but they plundered the rebels, as well. Which would not have concerned Abram too much, except that one of the captives they took just so happened to be Lot, as he was a resident of Sodom at the time.

However, before going any further on this story, one has to remember that the reputations of Sodom and Gomorrah had already proceeded them. Everybody who was a neighbor to these people in that particular region knew that the people of Sodom and Gomorrah were among the most wicked and corrupt of all peoples on the Earth. To give the proper perspective, it would be like walking through Eight Mile in the city of Detroit or walking through one of the rough neighborhoods in New York City, except that whereas Detroit's and New York City's troublemakers mainly entail just the gangs that live there, you're talking about everybody living in Sodom and Gomorrah who were rotten to the core.

Still, Abram's concern over the safety of his nephew Lot trumped any thoughts about the reputation of Sodom and Gomorrah. So much so, in fact, that he even rounded up an entire army to defeat Kedorlaomer and his troops. Yes, the odds seemed to be great against Abram, especially since Kedorlaomer had just defeated five different kingdoms all at once. However, Abram was the type of man you did not want to mess with, especially if you wanted to do harm to one of his relatives, and with God's supernatural protection, he found a way to not only defeat Kedorlaomer but also rescue Lot in the process.

After the events of Abram freeing his nephew Lot, many years would go by, with some key events going on. For instance, the defeat of Kedorlaomer resulted in Abram being blessed and honored by Melchizedek, who at the time was the main priest of God Most High, and also the king of Salem, later to be known as Jerusalem. Also, since Sarai was barren at the time, Abram thought that maybe his heir would not be conceived by Sarai but by her maidservant from Egypt Hagar. Hagar did conceive and bore to Abram Ishmael, but even though Ishmael would end up becoming prosperous, and his descendants ended up as a great nation, Ishmael was not the chosen one by God. That was to come later, but in the meantime, it was 13 years after Ishmael's birth that the practice of circumcision was practiced for the first time, and it started with Abram, Ishmael, and their relatives being the first people to do so. Then, in Genesis, chapter 18, the fate of not only Abram and Sarai but also Sodom and Gomorrah was revealed, and it was revealed by three seemingly ordinary strangers.

Just before this news was revealed, however, Abram was called by God to change both his and Sarai's identities. Abram from now on was to be known as Abraham, and Sarai would be known as Sarah. There was a reason for this: Abraham is a name that means "father of many," and while both Sarai and Sarah mean "princess," the name Sarah was at the time reserved for mothers. That was significant because at the time, Sarah was still barren, and Abraham was nearing 100 years old. Yet what God was doing, at least in my opinion, was reprogramming Abraham and Sarah's states of mind so that they would start to think prosperous thoughts instead of thoughts of failure.

Now, on to Genesis 18. Three men appeared to Abraham near his tent, except these three seemingly innocent strangers were no ordinary men. At least two of these "men" were in reality angels sent by God, and the third one is strongly believed to be the Lord Himself.

Except Abraham did not know this at the time; he still thought they were just men who had traveled a great distance. In the New International Version Study Bible, Abraham refered to one of the men as "my lord." When referring to someone as your lord, you are showing respect for someone who is superior to you. However, if you noticed, when Abraham referred to one of the men as his lord, the word "lord" is not capitalized. By the text being written the way it is, Abraham was still giving the respect one would with another man; however, by the word "lord" not being capitalized, it was made clear that Abraham did not realize that one of the men that he was talking to was, in fact, his deity.

Anyway, Abraham still showed hospitality to his guests, the way any man would have in that time period. He had Sarah make bread for them, and some water was brought out to them so that they could wash their feet. After all, these men had traveled a great distance, Abraham thought, and not only must they be hungry, but the desert sands must have been torturous on their feet. All seemed to be going well and normal. At least it did, until these supposed strangers got to the point of why they were here to visit Abraham and Sarah.

While the three men were eating, they asked Abraham where Sarah was. Abraham, I am sure, looked at them a little curiously, in part because he did not know why they wanted to know of Sarah's whereabouts, but also because they knew her name—this, in spite of the fact that Abraham had never revealed this information to them. Still, Abraham did tell them that she was in their tent. What was written next is interesting for two reasons.

First, the next statement made in the Bible was made by someone known as "The Lord" (Genesis 18:3). Why not just say that "one of the men said..."? Why was the next speaker referred to as "The Lord"? It had to be that God Himself was speaking to Abraham about was to happen, but that He was revealed to Abraham in human form. The second interesting thing was what "The Lord" said. He stated the following: "I will return to you about this time next year, and Sarah...shall have a son" (Genesis 18:10). Abraham had heard of such promises before, but here was the difference: this time it was revealed not only that Sarah would provide Abraham with a son but also when this was to take place. Remember, at this time Abraham was 99 years old, and Sarah was 89, yet according to "The Lord," they were to have a son the following year. Boy, that would be an exciting yet scary time if someone were a first-time dad at 100, and many would consider giving birth at age 90 to be unfathomable.

Needless to say, Sarah thought that such news was hysterical, and she, of course, laughed. "Come on, guys", Sarah thought to herself. "There is no way that I will be giving birth to a child, especially when I have been barren for almost nine decades." The Lord heard this and asked why Sarah laughed at this statement. Did she have doubts about what the Lord could do, that He could bring such a miracle into her life? Sarah tried to deny this, and she also now knew who was speaking to both her and Abraham, but the Lord knew better. Yes, Sarah, you did laugh at this news.

The next thing revealed to Abraham concerned the fate of Sodom and Gomorrah. Since the time that Abraham had freed Lot from his captors, things had gotten even worse than before in that region. Yes, in freeing Lot, Abraham also had to free those who were natives of Sodom and Gomorrah. However, instead of turning to the God that Abraham had worshipped, the people in these two towns seemed to only increase and multiply in the abominations that they had committed. It was now the Lord's mission to find out if the abominations that these people had been committing now warranted their destruction, even though I am sure He already knew the answer to this.

Abraham was terrified at this thought, but it was not because he cared about what happened in Sodom and Gomorrah. If anything, he agreed that the people in those towns were wicked and full of evil. However, he was concerned about his nephew Lot, who for some reason returned there. "Far be it, Lord, that you wipe out the righteous along with the wicked." Abraham countered, "Should not the Earth's rightful Judge do what is right?"

At this point, Abraham began to bargain God down in hopes of saving his nephew Lot.

First, Abraham asked if the cities were to be saved if the Lord found 50 righteous people. Yes, they would be spared for their sake. Well, Lord, what about 40? Yes, the city would be saved for the sake of the 40. What if there were 30 righteous people, or maybe even as few as 20? Even for the sake of 20 righteous people, the Lord would not destroy Sodom and Gomorrah. Eventually, Abraham got it down to the number 10, and even if only 10 righteous people were to be found, the Lord would still spare those cities along the Jordan River. I believe that God allowed Abraham to bargain for people's lives like this because He held Abraham, who most certainly was a righteous man, in such high regard. I certainly do not think that God would allow someone who was unfaithful to God to have a chance to bargain the way Abraham did. Now, the question became, did the Lord find even 10 righteous people in the land of Sodom and Gomorrah?

Well, when the angels arrived in the town of Sodom, the first person they found was Lot, and it was obvious that Lot, thankfully, had not joined in with the practices that most of the people in Sodom and Gomorrah were committing. After all, if Lot had practiced such abominable acts, why was it that he would care for what he thought of at the time to be mere men? Why would he be so insistent upon making sure that these "strangers" who came by and visited him did not go into the town square? So, the two men, who were really God's angels, stopped at Lot's house for a little bit and ate with him and his family.

Many people in the world have some idea of where the word sodomy comes from, that it originated from the town of Sodom. However, they also do not understand why the homosexual lifestyle is seen as wrong not by just the Christian faith but also the faiths of most religions in the world today. Apparently, someone noticed the two angels coming into Lot's house and then made mention of this to everyone in the town. Three things to remember here: first, that the whole town was in agreement of what to do with these "strangers" who showed up in their town. Second, so far, Lot, his wife, and their two daughters, were considered to be righteous people. That meant that with four people down, only another six people who did not participate in the abominable practices known about in that town were needed to spare Sodom and Gomorrah. Last, like Lot, the people in Sodom did not think of these "strangers" as anything more than real men, and it was this fact that would prove to be the most crucial part of this story.

So, what was the first thing that the men of Sodom wanted to do with God's angels? Did they host a banquet for them, or greet them like Abraham had done earlier, or even treat them with any sort of respect or dignity? No, they did not! Instead, the male residents of Sodom wanted to have sexual relations with these "wanderers." Yes, you read that right; the men of Sodom wanted sex with God's angels, even though the men of Sodom did not know that these were God's angels, and it was because you had men from Sodom who wanted sexual relations with those whom they thought were merely human, and you had a town in total agreement, for that matter; that is why the word sodomy exist today, why both Sodom and Gomorrah were condemned to destruction today, and why gay marriage and homosexuality should be considered for what they have been considered by most major religions; at least under Christianity, while repentance and forgiveness is possible, those are nothing more than an abomination for those who continue such practices.

Of course, there are other Bible verses that deal with this issue as well. Leviticus 18:22 states that homosexual behavior is what I described earlier, and that is an abomination. The apostle Paul also made mention, in 1 Corinthians 6:9, that among those who will not inherit the kingdom of God were homosexuals, and he was consistent in his message that such people would be punished by God, as seen in Romans 1:26–27. There was also the story of how the people in the town of Gibeah, who were of the tribe of Benjamin, in Judges 19:22–23, wanted to have sexual relations with a male Levite who stopped by their town, but the owner of the place where the Levite was stopping by told these men to not do such a vile and disgraceful thing, which tells you that such practice was, and still is, wrong.

Anyway, the people of Sodom did not stop with just wanting unnatural sexual relations with God's angels, but they also wanted Lot to pay. Why? Because Lot had dared to try and stop them, and they felt it was wrong for a foreigner like Lot to all of a sudden pass judgment on them. Gee, I wonder what movement today would make a similar statement...However, just before something terrible was about to happen to Lot and his family, the Lord's angels pulled him back and blinded the residents of Sodom, thus making safe passage for Lot and his family. At that, the angels told Lot that he, his wife, and his two daughters should leave right away. If Lot had any other relatives, as well, he should get them out also, or at least make an effort to do so. Lot, of course, obeyed this command and tried to warn his would-be sons-in-law, who also were in town, about the disaster that was about to take place. However, the men who had proposed to marry Lot's daughters did not heed the warning; they thought that Lot was either crazy or pulling some kind of rib, or perhaps was even in denial.

So, it ended up being just Lot, along with his wife and two daughters, who would leave Sodom before the impending destruction of both that town and Gomorrah. Furthermore, the angels added that Lot and his family must flee to the mountains and not look back, or else they too would be consumed. Lot pleaded that going to the mountains would take everything out of him and his family and asked they would be allowed to stay in a nearby town. The angels allowed this but warned that Lot and his family must hurry, for the Lord's hand would stave off destruction until they got to that town, which later on became known as Zoar, but also that Sodom and Gomorrah had to be destroyed soon.

Lot and his family did make it to Zoar, and it was at that moment that God destroyed Sodom and Gomorrah for their great wickedness with sulfuric fire and brimstone. Lot's wife, however, made the crucial mistake of disobeying God when she turned back to watch the city of Sodom be destroyed. Of course, as many would know, as soon as Lot's wife did so, she was turned into a pillar of salt. Many might think of this as impossible, since if she had succumbed to this condition by merely turning around, then Lot and his two daughters should have as well. However, I think that all of this could have happened, especially when you consider the direction of the winds on that fateful day. I mean, if you were warned by a credible source about sulfuric material coming down from the sky, wouldn't you want to move as far away as you could? Also, since Lot and his family were warned not to look back, that meant that the wind was blowing on their backs. By turning back, though, to face the city of Sodom, Lot's wife now had her face towards the wind, instead of away from it, and since that wind now carried extremely powerful sulfuric air with it, that meant that she was now breathing it; now her lungs were filled with the toxins, she was unable to move, and in the end you had a woman turned into a salty statue! Heh, heh!

There was a twist to this story, and it would, for a few centuries, cause much grief and heartache to the ancient Israelites. Once Lot and his daughters renewed their strength, they did leave Zoar and move to the mountains. Remember, by this time, Lot was now an old man, and his two daughters had nobody to continue their family lineage, which was very important in ancient times, since their main sources to do so, their spouses-to-be, refused to leave Sodom before its destruction. So the older daughter came up with a diabolical idea of getting their father Lot drunk to where he was more than just three sheets to the wind and, in fact, didn't know who was there or where he was. Once this happened, the older daughter had sex with her old man, and the following day, they did the same thing for the younger sister (why they could not just say hi to someone not related to them and go from there is beyond me). Anyway, what happened was that as a result of this sickening idea of incest, the two daughters ended up having their father's children (yeah, I need a puke bag too). The reason why this would be a problem for the Israelites later on was because the older daughter gave birth to a boy named Moab, and the younger daughter gave birth to Ben-Ammi. Later on, they would form the people of the Moabites and Ammonites, sworn enemies of Israel who, ironically, would be the children of Abraham. Talk about your family feuds.

As for Abraham, he did, of course, end up with a son through Sarah named Isaac, which means "laughter," which is interesting since Sarah earlier laughed at the notion of having a child. Well, there was enmity for a little bit between Ishmael and Isaac, and Abraham did have to send Ishmael and Hagar away. But don't worry—they did make it. Before his life concluded, however, Abraham had one final test of faith. God asked Abraham to kill his only son Isaac, and at this Abraham must have been extremely distraught. After all that he and Sarah went through, and God had promised Abraham that he would be the father of many nations, now God was asking him to sacrifice someone who was the most precious thing in his life? But, like so many times, Abraham's thinking was "Well, if God wanted this to happen, I must trust His judgment," and so, Abraham took Isaac up on a long journey, claiming that he must make a sacrifice to the Lord. What he did not tell his servants, or his wife Sarah, was that Isaac was to be the sacrifice. So, Abraham made all of the preparations, tied Isaac up, and was about to slay him (which, by the way, shows you what a brave boy Isaac must have been) when an angel of the Lord appeared to stop him. God now had his answer: that Abraham had not forsaken his faith in God, nor had he withheld Isaac from God's hand. Interestingly, it was very similar to how God was willing to give up Jesus, His only Son, in order to save humanity. Yes, sometimes we have to make the painful decision to let go of what we believe to be precious in our live, but if we are willing to stay in faith in God, our reward for such decisions will be great.

Chapter 4

Free at Last
(Books of Exodus, Leviticus, Numbers, and Deuteronomy)

Some years after Abraham and Sarah had their son Isaac, Isaac grew up, married Rebekah, and end up with two sons, twins, in fact. One was Esau, and the other was Jacob. Jacob, of course, later was to be renamed Israel and had twelve sons, one of whom, Joseph, became a great leader in Egypt. Even though the other brothers had conspired against Joseph years earlier, he still provided for their needs when he became the leader of the Egyptians under Pharaoh; all the while there was a great famine throughout the known world, and it even allowed them to stay on the land when they decided to bring their father Jacob with them. Even after Joseph and his brothers died, the people of Israel were growing and lived very well in the land of Egypt.

At a certain point, though, the Egyptians started to see the Israelites not as special guests in their land; no, they saw the Israelites as a growing military threat. Never mind that the Israelites were nothing but gracious for all that they had received from Egypt. Now was the time, in the minds of the Egyptians, for these Hebrew foreigners in the midst of their land to pay with their sweat and their tears. In other words, enslave them.

There might be a key reason for this. It was mentioned that a new king rose in Egypt, one who did not know Joseph (Exodus 1:8+note). Now, the people who ruled over Egypt before this new king obviously were fond of the Israelites, and the reason for this was how Joseph made Egypt the most prosperous nation in the world. It also did not hurt any that the rulers in Egypt around that time were mainly Semitic, so, in a way, they kind of did feel like kin to the Israelites. What is interesting is that at the time of the new king mentioned in Exodus 1:8, there was an uprising in Egypt, one that ushered in a new dynasty in Egypt while destroying those who knew Joseph. In fact, it is very likely that this king, or Pharaoh, was Ahmose, known as the man who founded Egypt's 18th dynasty, and if that was the case, then not only would Egypt's old rulers suffer but it would make sense that those whom they helped, like the Israelites, would be seen as a threat, as well.

Now, you are no doubt wondering why, if this new Pharaoh saw the Israelites as a threat, would he not just go ahead and slaughter all of them right then and there. What is forgotten, however, is that while I am sure many people in Egypt did not like the fact that the Israelites were prospering on their land, and some might have even felt that it was at their expense, they also would most likely have not favored genocide on a people whose relative was Joseph. Also, let us not forget that one uprising could still have sprung up a counterrevolution movement if things were not handled properly, and committing genocide on a people favored by the previous regime would not have been the wisest decision. So, to weaken the Israelites, or at least to ensure they did not collaborate with the new Pharaoh's enemies, this new king of Egypt thought it would be wise to enslave them for the time being.

However, it became very obvious that merely enslaving the Israelites would not weaken them, and if anything, they multiplied in numbers even more. No matter how much Pharaoh oppressed them, the Israelites were still producing more of their kind. It was then that the king of Egypt took a desperate action, something that would mortify even the worst of human beings.

For what Pharaoh told the Israelite midwives was that if the child born was a girl, let it live, but if the Hebrew child was a boy, kill it. Obviously, this was very cruel on the part of the Egyptian king, but it also was very flawed as well. Why would an Israelite midwife, whose people were still on a mission to populate the world and grow, kill any, much less all, male children based on the whims of a foreign ruler? I am sorry, but there was no way anybody would be committing genocide on their own people, especially when it was being forced upon them by someone else. So, not shockingly, the midwives lied to Pharaoh and told him that the children were being born before they could arrive in order to determine the child's gender. Lying is generally the wrong thing to do, like when you say that everything is going great in school when, in reality, you are failing three different subjects, or if you say that you have a free day, in spite of the fact that you have five different things going on in that particular day. I think, however, that lying to someone in order to prevent the genocide of your own people is something that falls within the lines of acceptable behavior.

So, not shockingly, Pharaoh turned to his own people to carry out this terrible deed that the Israelite midwives refused to do. What was fascinating, however, was that Pharaoh was willing to kill the male children, but he was willing to let the female children live. There were two reasons for this. First, a female can only get pregnant once at a time. She can only get pregnant a second time after a child is born, unless the woman is a metaphysical fluke. Men, on the other hand, can get as many women knocked up as they can, and their reproductive systems can last a lifetime. Hence, the theory behind Pharaoh's twisted logic was that if you had less men around, that meant fewer children were being born.

The second reason may or may not be as obvious, but it will disgust the feminists of today. Egypt, like everywhere

47

else, was a male-dominated society that treated women more like property than people. The thinking here was that if you wanted to strengthen your own people while weakening another race, it would have been easier at the time to control women of your own people for the sole purpose of procreation than it would men, even if the people you were controlling were of a race that you were enslaving. Basically, an Egyptian man could produce a child with an Israelite woman and still call it his own, but if an Egyptian woman tried the same thing with a Hebrew male, you would have all-out war on your hands, and nobody would accept such a proposition.

It was in such a time period that Moses was born to Levite parents; only when he was born, his parents could not name him anything. They were so afraid of the Egyptians and what they might do to the baby should they find him. So, at first, they tried to hide the baby within the confines of their home, but it was pretty obvious that this was not going to work too well. So, Moses's parents devised an idea where they would hide the baby in a papyrus basket and send it onto the Nile River. While the basket was traveling on the Nile, Moses's sister Miriam kept a close eye on it to see what would happen.

Well, it just so happened that the daughter of Pharaoh was bathing in that same Nile River along with her attendants. One of the slave girls noticed a basket coming in their direction, and when Pharaoh's daughter opened it up, she found a Hebrew child inside it, the same one whose parents were trying to hide for the first three months of the boy's life. Now, think about this: the child was being hidden by his parents so that Pharaoh and his men would not kill the baby, but eventually they had to put the baby in a basket and send it down the Nile, only to be found by a slave of the daughter of the man they were trying to hide the baby from in the first place. If there was a golden opportunity to kill a child of a race that you wanted to commit genocide upon, this would be it. Talk about a nightmare of a scenario!

Before I go any further, though, you might be wondering why, if the Hebrew people of that time did not want their male children killed, did they not fight back against the Egyptians. The only thing I could compare this to, I guess, would be the Holocaust. In that situation, part of the reason why the Holocaust happened was because of Hitler's unyielding and oppressive hatred of the Jews, and a good chunk of the blame deserves to fall on men like Neville Chamberlain, who tried appeasement in an attempt to contain Hitler, when they would have been better standing up to him before such an atrocity could have taken place, but also, part of the reason why the Holocaust happened, believe it or not, was because the Jewish people, for the longest time, <u>did not</u> <u>fight back</u>. You see, the Jewish people were told by the Nazis that if they obeyed orders and cooperated, their lives might be spared. They could not comprehend that the Nazis had zero intention of letting them live. Hence, there was no way, when the Axis powers, especially Germany, were winning World War II, before the United States joined in, that the Jewish people were going to resist what was perceived to be, at that time, the strongest military power in the world. This, in my opinion, might have been similar to the scenario when the Israelites were enslaved in Egypt. *

Now, back to Pharaoh's daughter. Here was this Hebrew child her father commanded to be killed. So, what did Pharaoh's daughter do? Did she have the child executed? No, she felt sorry and sympathetic towards the baby, and had his mother nurse him until the time was right for Pharaoh's daughter to raise him to be an Egyptian, and because she drew the child out of the water, Pharaoh's daughter was the one to name the kid Moses.

Moses then grew up, learning about the customs of the Egyptians. He probably was schooled in learning the language, exposed to their customs and their gods, and since many thought that he was the son of Pharaoh's daughter, was probably exposed to how to rule and govern Egypt. That was, until Moses was 40 years of age. For what happened next was that Moses saw an Egyptian whipping and abusing one of the Hebrew slaves. What was strange was that Moses had compassion for the slave. Now, Moses may have been a Levite by blood, but he never knew that. All Moses knew was how the Egyptians were supposed to run things, and for that matter, he even thought that he was an Egyptian. The fact that he stopped the Egyptian slave driver from doing any more damage was indeed unique. In doing so, however, Moses might have gone a bit too far, and instead of merely reprimanding the slave driver, Moses, killed him and hid his body in the Egyptian sand.

Needless to say, it did not take long for rumors to spread about what Moses had done to the slave driver. The following day, two Hebrew men were fighting each other. Maybe they had some sort of argument over responsibilities, or maybe they just did not get along. Whatever the case, Moses noticed the fight and asked the instigator in the brawl why he would strike his fellow Hebrew man. The instigator responded, first by asking Moses if he was now going to pass judgement on him; then the instigator asked Moses if he would deliver the same fate to him as Moses had done the day before to one of the Egyptians. It was right then and there that Moses knew that if Pharaoh had not found out about what transpired the previous day, he was going to really soon. When that happened, Moses was going to be chased around until he was caught and later on executed. Somehow, killing a fellow Egyptian to save a Hebrew slave's life was something I am sure Pharaoh did not take too kindly; thus Moses ran away before the Egyptians could catch up and execute the punishment they had for him. At that point in time,

Moses did not know that the first third of his life had already passed.

If the first 40 years in the life of Moses was about growing up and living in Egyptian luxury, the next 40 years were about self-discovery. It was while Moses was a runaway fugitive in the wilderness that he noticed some girls in trouble. Shepherds in the area drove them away when they tried to water their father's sheep. Moses, knowing that the shepherds were in the wrong, drove them out and helped water the flock that the girls were trying to water themselves. When the father of the girls, who was a Midian priest by the name of Reuel (also known as Jethro), found out what happened, he invited Moses over to his house. Moses was given Reuel's daughter Zipporah to be his wife, and they raised a son together. Moses might not have been as prosperous as he was when he was perceived to be the next great ruler of Egypt, but Moses did have some security and a job as one of Reuel's shepherds. God knew, however, that He had plans for Moses that did not involve only tending to Reuel's sheep. The cry of the Israelites was at an all-time high, and they were begging and pleading for a deliverer. Moses thought that he might have had safe haven, but he still did not fully understand who he was, and there just so happened to be a strange glow coming out of one of the mountains in Reuel's region that had the curiosity and attention of Moses.

Moses, upon seeing a fire on top of Horeb, also known as the mountain of God, went up towards it, because he wanted to know why, in spite of the fire, the bush that was lit up did not burn out. Many people thought that this would be nonsense, but, in fact, there was a rare gas plant that was a variation of Fraxinella, or the Latin version, *Dictamnus Albus L,* within the same region that Moses resided during his time as a shepherd of his father-in-law's sheep that had a certain oil in it that made the plant flammable, but, like the Human Torch of Fantastic Four fame, its outer layers were able to withstand the flames. In this case, however, God appeared to Moses within the flames, and He had a very important message to give to Moses.

One of the first things God told Moses was very interesting, for He told Moses that He was not only the God of Moses's father but also the God of Abraham, of Isaac, and of Jacob. Moses, as pointed out earlier, grew up in the culture and worship of the Egyptians. There was no talk of what God did for Abraham, the dreams of Jacob and Joseph, no mention of how Isaac found his wife Rebekah, and if there was any mention of this at all, it was by the Israelites, and Moses was programmed to believe that he was Egyptian, not a Hebrew man. Even when living under Jethro's roof, he saw himself as nothing more than a drifter from Egypt or, maybe at worst, a traitor to his class and nation. Now, here was this God, whom Moses had heard about only through Hebrew slaves and possibly Jethro's family, since they were descendants of Ishmael telling him that Moses's father did not worship one of the pharaohs but rather Jehovah Himself. This alone would have been hard to take.

There was more, however. God also told Moses that he, the man who was raised in the life of the Egyptians, was going to free their Hebrew slaves from this cruel tyranny. First, God convinced Moses by telling him that He would be with Moses on this journey and that on this very mountain where Moses was standing was where to worship God once they were free from Egypt. Second, God gave Moses His name that should be called to those who wonder by what authority Moses had been sent to free them. Well, it was somewhat of a name. That name was I AM who I AM. This was to let the Jewish people know that Moses was representing the one God whom they could trust and rely upon.

Moses was still reluctant about this journey that God was sending him on, so God showed him signs that he was supposed to do in front of the Israelites if His name alone did not convince them. Signs such as turning the rod given to Moses into a snake, changing back and forth between normal hands and leprous ones, and turning water from the Nile to blood once it reached dry land. You would think that Moses, after seeing all this, would be willing to serve the Lord and get His people out of Egypt right then and there, but amazingly, Moses was still making excuses as to why he was not the man to lead God's chosen people, stating that he had never been eloquent in speech. By now, I am sure that the Lord was getting a little more than just agitated by the lack of faith shown by Moses and mentioned to Moses that he had a brother named Aaron, who was looking for him and who also happened to be an exceptional speaker in his own right. Aaron was to be the mouthpiece for Moses, and it was after this that Moses finally ran out of excuses. He was going to follow God's lead in getting the Israelites out of Egypt, even though I am still sure he believed that the Egyptians would execute him for murdering a fellow Egyptian and for being a fugitive afterwards. Little did Moses know at the time that at the ripe old age of 80, he still had another 40 years to live, and those last 40 years were to be the most eventful in his life. That's right; instead of retirement on a 401k plan, Moses was going to be doing what he was called to do.

First, Moses and Aaron did meet each other, and once they did, they followed God's orders to show the Israelites that, yes, God did indeed send Moses to free His own people from the oppressive regime of the Egyptians. However, when Moses told Pharaoh to let God's people go, so that they could worship Him, Pharaoh just laughed. By this time, Pharaoh did not even know that the God of the Israelites existed; why should he let the slaves of his kingdom loose in order to worship someone who was persona non grata in Pharaoh's mind? Instead, Pharaoh made more oppressive orders fall upon the Israelites, which mainly consisted of, yes, the Israelites had to make bricks, but now, instead of having straw given to them, the Israelites had to find the straw on their own, and they had to meet the same quota of brick as they did before.

In order to appreciate the importance of straw in those times, in regards to brickmaking, one must realize how bricks were made. Yes, you could make bricks with just clay. However, clay has a tendency to break easily, especially under harsh weather conditions. However, if you add straw into the mix, and if the clay and straw were mixed together just right, you have bricks that are stronger and more durable. This was especially important because before Pharaoh made this edict, straw was given to Israelite foremen to make the bricks (Exodus 5:7+note). Now that straw would not be provided, it made things harder because the foremen were never shown where to get straw.

Needless to say, the Israelite foremen were not happy to be mistreated by Pharaoh's slave drivers, and they let Moses and Aaron hear about it. However, the Lord did tell Moses in Exodus 3:19 that Pharaoh would not listen unless he was compelled by a mighty hand. Such a task would require faith and perseverance. Furthermore, Moses had to start believing that such a mission could be done successfully, which was a struggle unto itself. Moses might have made the familiar excuse of being a faulty speaker, except that by now he realized that the Israelites were so filled with a feeling of hopelessness, and if this mission was to be successful, Moses had to get out of his own self-pity and start believing that God not only could get the Israelites out of Egypt but, if Moses and the people start believing, that He would.

Of course, everyone knows what happened next. Moses and Aaron first showed God's power to Pharaoh by throwing Moses's walking stick onto the ground, and when they did so, the staff turned into a snake. Pharaoh's magicians could do the same trick, but Moses's snake ate the two snakes made by the magicians. Pharaoh probably should have known better, but he didn't. It was going to take more than a mere magician's trick to convince Pharaoh that it might be wise to let the Israelites go, even if Moses did get the upper hand in this exchange. Thus, the next event was the start of the 10 plagues in Egypt.

The first two plagues, the turning of the Nile River into blood and the teeming of the frogs in Egypt, were pretty bad, but Pharaoh was still not too concerned, since his magicians could do the same trick, but it was the third plague, the one about the gnats, that got some attention, since Pharaoh's magicians could not duplicate that one with their dark and secret arts. The fourth plague, though, with the flies, was where God made a distinction between His people and the people of Egypt. The Israelites, who resided in the town of Goshen, were spared from the plagues, but the Egyptians were now the ones feeling God's wrath.

At this point, Pharaoh was at least willing to consider a compromise, such as letting the Israelites worship their God, but to do it within the confines of Egypt. Still, as soon as one of the plagues would end, Pharaoh would change his mind and state that the Hebrew people were to stay put. Two plagues would follow, with the death of Egyptian livestock and the boils and sores covering the bodies of every Egyptian. These were really bad, but because Pharaoh hardened his heart, the next three plagues were to be even worse.

First, there was the hailstorm that covered Egypt, and it was the worst one that ever happened. Now, the crops that the Egyptians planted were being destroyed, which just showed you the difference between serving God, as the Egyptians did when they had Joseph to give direction, and disobeying Him and hardening your heart, as this Pharaoh was now doing. If the hailstorm was not bad enough, the next plague, the one of the locusts, was even harder on the Egyptians because locusts eat plants right to the very edge of the ground. More concessions followed from Pharaoh, only to be reversed again once the plagues ended, but it was the ninth plague, the land of Egypt being covered in darkness for three days, that should have told Pharaoh that if he did not let the Israelites go, then something worse was going to happen. Instead, Pharaoh threatened Moses, saying that if Moses and Pharaoh met again, Moses was going to lose his life.

At this point, there was a reason why Pharaoh made this statement to Moses. Quite frankly, Moses's God had delivered a butt-whooping of mammoth proportions to the land of Egypt; so much so, in fact, that it humbled Egypt's proud king. To make things even worse for Pharaoh, all of this was being done in front of his family, friends, and advisors. This was a problem to Pharaoh because pharaohs at that time were not only considered to be rulers of the land of Egypt but they were considered gods as well. Gods do not humble themselves; they are the ones who are supposed to humble others. However, with nine plagues that had already happened in Egypt, some people in the land might think that this Pharaoh was no god at all, which really made Pharaoh angry, and that was why he threatened the life of Moses.

What Pharaoh did not know at that time, however, was that God was about to deliver the ultimate kick in the gut to him. In ancient times, the firstborn child was the most precious thing in a man's life, especially if it was a son. Whatever happened to the firstborn was a reflection of his father. If the firstborn did well, that was good news, but if he did something terrible, or if he ended up being poor, that sent a bad message about his father. What happened next, however, was the worst possible thing that could have happened to Pharaoh.

One day, the Lord told Moses to have each house where the Israelites lived covered around the doors with sheep's blood. This was to be crucial, since it would help the angel of death make a distinction between the Israelites and the Egyptians. This way, the Hebrew families would lose none of their firstborns, whereas the Egyptians would not fare nearly as well. Of course, with this signifying Israel's first Passover, there were certain rituals that had to be done, but the main thing was that the angel of death passed over the houses of the Israelites and slaughtered all of the firstborns of Egypt. No riches in the world could stop this, and the angel of death even killed Pharaoh's firstborn child, his only son, and it was this 10th and final plague that finally broke Pharaoh's will.

What was interesting, however, was that Pharaoh himself did not die. Why was that, especially when in most situations of that era it was the firstborn who took over the kingdom once their father died? I for one can only think of one of two possibilities: either this Pharaoh had an older brother who died without having any children, possibly in battle, or maybe God wanted this Pharaoh to live in order to see with his eyes the true power of God. In either case, though, by losing his firstborn son, Pharaoh had now lost face value and did, in fact, grant Moses an audience—not to kill him, though, but to let the Israelites go, under the exact same conditions that God and Moses demanded from him. After the Israelites left, however, Pharaoh and his officers realized that their slaves were gone, that they had lost their meal ticket. In doing so, they also decided that they were to seek out Israelite blood for what happened to their firstborns. Ironically, in pursuit of Hebrew people dying by their hand, the Egyptians were the ones who lost their lives, all without the Israelites firing a single shot.

Two things should be noted here. The first thing is that the quickest way to get from Egypt to the promised land that God intended to give to the Israelites was to travel through the northern edge of what is now known as the Sinai Peninsula. Instead, the Israelites went through the Red Sea and the southern tip of the Sinai Peninsula. Which part of the Red Sea the Israelites crossed was uncertain; however, the reason why they did not go north was because the land of Canaan at that time was loaded with all sorts of peoples, with the Philistines in particular starting to come into their own. If they saw a people coming into their land who were free because of divine intervention, they would perceive these people as a threat that must be destroyed, and at that time, the people of Israel were nowhere near ready for battle, either in terms of having a standing army or being ready mentally.

The other thing that was interesting was that among other things, Moses and the Israelites brought with them the body of Joseph, or should I say his bones. Yes, this was the same Joseph who was Jacob's son, as well as the second-in-command in all of Egypt. It was amazing because Joseph served under a regime whereby the pharaoh at that time was kind to the Israelites, and this current regime was one that did nothing but oppress the Hebrew people and wanted them gone before the nation of Israel would come into being. So, it is mind-boggling as to why this pharaoh, who treated the Israelites like dirt when they were his slaves, would not just discard Joseph's body, or at the very least, hide it in a location where nobody, especially the Israelites, could find it.

Well, once Pharaoh and his friends and advisors realized that no slaves were left to build them anything, the Egyptians knew that they would have to do all the work, and actually working themselves instead of having slaves do it for them was unacceptable. So, Pharaoh came with 600 chariots strong, in order to capture, and most likely kill, 600,000 Hebrew men, as well as scores more of women and children. You would think that the Israelites would have the numbers advantage based on how many were there, but remember that Pharaoh had brought with him professionally trained soldiers. They were used to killing people and winning battles, whereas the Israelites had known nothing but slavery. Also, keep in mind that the Egyptians probably had the most advanced weaponry of that era, whereas the Israelites had, what, pickaxes and shovels, if even that.

It certainly seemed like Moses had made a tactical blunder that even the least experienced of generals would not have made. How were the Israelites to survive while being trapped among Pharaoh and his army and the Red Sea? If you tried to run away, you would drown in the Red Sea; try to stand your ground and fight, and you were going up against what was the most powerful military in the world, and they were hell-bent on killing you, which was something they were most likely to succeed at. What the Israelites had on their side, however, though most of them did not know it at the time, was a God who mastered at making the impossible happen.

First, God made a cloud of fire to separate the Egyptians from the Hebrew people. Then, with Moses using his staff and spreading his arms wide, He parted the Red Sea, giving the Israelites safe passage to walk. Once all the Hebrew people had passed, the cloud of fire was lifted. Pharaoh foolishly thought that it was safe to pursue once more, but he and his army rode straight into a trap that God had designed. For once Pharaoh and his chariots got to the pathway God had created for the Israelites, the waters from the Red Sea collapsed on them. Pharaoh and his men either drowned or were crushed by the waves, whereas the Israelites, on the other side of the Red Sea now, were saved.

Unfortunately, God's miracles did not translate into the Israelite people having faith and gratitude in their divine helper. Be it manna from heaven, quail to eat, water springing forth from rocks, or any other miracles that God had done, nothing seemed to satisfy these people. Moses did receive the 10 Commandments, probably because he was their leader but also because of his sense of justice, in my opinion, only to find out that the Israelites were worshipping a golden calf, which caused him to be so enraged that he destroyed the original 10 Commandments. Thankfully, God was merciful enough to give Moses and the Israelites another set, with the same exact words attached to them.

Unfortunately, the first Israelites who were freed from Egypt might have sealed their own fates when Moses sent 12 spies, each one representing one of the 12 tribes of Israel, to explore the land of Canaan, which was to be their promised land. Not only did 10 of the 12 spies say that the peoples there were unconquerable but that they also later on spread false rumors to the rest of the Hebrew people, saying that the land was filled with poor vegetation, as stated in Numbers 13. This resulted in many getting bitten by cobras, and most only survived when God told Moses to produce a bronze serpent and commanded the people to look up to it so that they might live. Even Moses himself faltered, and because he would not give God the glory at the waters of Meribah Kadesh (Deuteronomy 21:35), he was still allowed to see the promised land, but he could not go to it. Yes, the people of

Israel were freed from their Egyptian taskmasters during the Exodus, but it took another 40 years in the wilderness for them to act like a nation.

* Information can be seen in the book Revolution, copyright 2000, by Michael Brown pg. 260. Published by Regal Books.

Chapter 5
True Leadership
(Book of Joshua)

Moses, the man who led the Israelites through the travels of the wilderness for 40 years, and who freed his own brethren out of Egyptian slavery, was now dead. The Israelites were close to reaching the promised land, but the Jordan River was still between them and their goal. Scores of different peoples were on the other side of the Jordan River, all battle tested, and while the Israelites had face armies in their quest to reach the promised land, almost everyone who saw the 10 plagues in Egypt and experienced the Exodus were gone, all because they had zero faith in God; this, in spite of the fact that He had provided miracles for them on a daily basis. Who, now, could possibly lead this new generation to a land flowing with milk and honey when the previous generation had faltered?

The answer came in the form of a man known as Joshua, son of Nun! This was the man, who, along with Caleb, was one of the two spies who sent out a positive report on the land of Canaan and believeed that the

66

Israelites could defeat their enemies once they crossed the Jordan River. In a way, Joshua was also the general, so to speak, in all of the battles that the Israelites had fought against those who tried to prevent them from crossing the Jordan River. Unquestionably, Moses was the one who was the leader of the Israelites through the wilderness, but Joshua had some leadership qualities himself, especially in the heat of a battle. If Moses was the keeper of the law (and rightfully so), Joshua, in a way, was one who many could say was one of its enforcers. Anyway, after Moses died, the Lord Almighty Himself appeared to Joshua, telling him what lay ahead and how Joshua would not only lead the Hebrew people across the Jordan River but also lead them into victory over anybody who would dare stand in the way of the Israelites and their promised land. After that, the Lord told Joshua to be courageous, to have no fear, because the Lord would be there for Joshua, just as He had been there for Moses before him. There was one condition, though; the Lord told Joshua that all of these things would only happen if Joshua and the people of Israel obeyed the Lord's commands and kept His Laws. So, the only question that remained would be whether or not Joshua would pass the test that was set before him.

First thing was first, however. Joshua knew full well that once he and the Hebrew people crossed the Jordan River, which excluded here the women and children from the tribes of Reuben, Gad, and half a tribe of Manasseh, since the land east of the Jordan was promised to them on the condition that the men old enough to fight would help the rest of the Israelites gain possession of their lands, they would first encounter the people of Jericho. So, Joshua sent two spies to check out that city, especially their walls.

This was no easy mission, and for several good reasons. For one thing, it was believed at the time that Jericho's walls were impregnable. Also, even though the land of Canaan was, in reality, nothing more than a bunch of mini-kingdoms that controlled one, maybe two cities at the most, Jericho's kingdom was known for having well-trained soldiers, particularly when on the defensive. On top of that, though, the king of Jericho had already received word that the Israelites were heading in his direction. So, right off the bat, the Israelites did not even have the element of surprise.

Later on, it turned out that Jericho's king even knew that two spies were in his land when they were. Of course, he also had some idea that these spies were, in fact, searching the land. What the king of Jericho did not count on, however, was that the two spies were hiding right inside his walls, nor did he figure out that one of his subjects was helping them out, which just so happened to be the least likely person to do so, and it was because of this brave woman that Israel's mission considering Jericho ended up being so successfully done.

You see, in addition to Jericho's king, there was also a prostitute by the name of Rahab, who just so happened to notice the spies. In addition, it also turned out that Rahab had some valuable information to give to the spies. The Canaanites, and especially the residents of Jericho at the time, had heard about all the miracles that God had done for the Israelites, from the 10 plagues in Egypt, to the crossing of the Red Sea, to even the conquering of the Amorites mentioned in Numbers 21:21–35. Because of the successes that the Israelites had against their enemies, and because God was with them, the people of Jericho were already afraid of the Israelites even before any battle to place, and this was despite the advantages that Jericho seemed to have had. In fact, things had gotten so bad that at some point just before most of the Israelites had even crossed the Jordan River, Rahab herself had given up and turned away from the beliefs and gods that her fellow countrymen had believed in.

What I find interesting about all of this, however, is that the two Israelite spies did not take into any sort of consideration that Rahab was practicing the world's oldest profession. After all, this type of practice was an abomination according to God's chosen people when He condemned the act of adultery as was written on the 10 Commandments; according to such a law, the spies had every right to just go ahead and slaughter Rahab on the spot. Instead, they guaranteed Rahab and her family safe passage, as long as she told nobody of their whereabouts. It just shows you that even the lowest of people can be redeemed and saved if they just change their conduct, or do an act of kindness.

Meanwhile, Joshua and the Israelites faced a dilemma of their own: how to actually cross the Jordan River. Yes, it was possible to do such a thing; after all, when the Israelites needed to cross the Red Sea 40 years earlier, all that was needed was for Moses to hold his staff and spread his arms wide. There are, however, some differences that need to be pointed out.

For starters, Moses could do all sorts of miraculous events and signs because God needed Moses to be able to perceive a god-like image to Pharaoh, even if Moses himself never made such a claim, because Pharaoh only respected those he perceived to be immensely mighty or gods themselves. That way, it would become possible to force Pharaoh's hand into letting the Israelite slaves go. In the case of Joshua, however, God did not need him to be perceived as someone with supernatural capabilities. No, God just needed Joshua to be the sound general that he was and to also obey God's command.

Another, and a much more, significant thing to point out, is that Joshua had priests carrying the ark of the covenant. If you look back at Exodus 12:31–36, after the Passover and the slaughtering of the Egyptian firstborns by the angel of death, not only did the Egyptians let the

Israelites go but they also gave the Hebrew people some of their gold, silver, and all sorts of food and clothing. Why is this important, you may ask? Because that gold would be used in the construction of the ark of the covenant, as described in Exodus 37:1–9, and it just so happened that the ark was built long after the Israelites crossed the Red Sea.

So, you may ask, what was the significance of the ark itself? Because it was believed by the ancient Israelites to contain God's power, which was used in times of battle. Once Joshua and the Israelites knew not only of its power but also of the terms and conditions that had to be met in order to carry the ark into battle and to have its power be at its most effective, such as the fact that the Levites were the only ones allowed to carry the ark, and they had to do it while using beams made out of acacia wood that were supposed to be hooked to the sides of the ark, the Israelites were now ready to cross the Jordan River, with the Levites carrying the ark going first. Once all who were supposed to had crossed, Joshua had 12 men, each one carrying a stone, place those stones on the path that they crossed, in order to represent each of the 12 tribes of Israel.

Now, the stage was just about set for what was to happen to the Walls of Jericho. Two things happened, though, just before the Israelites actually arrived in Jericho. First, the Hebrew people had to be circumcised, as they were children of Abraham. This was because most of the people of Israel who were alive at the time of the battle against Jericho were not around during the Exodus from Egypt. They just so happened to have been born during the wilderness years, and since you were most likely not to have circumcision be the top of your to-do list if you were walking in the middle of nowhere, chances are you will not be circumcised until you reach your final destination. So, because of this fact, circumcision must happen first, so that the people may be pure before the battle begins.

Another interesting thing that happened was that one day a man in military garb appeared. Joshua, who didn't know what to make of this, asked the man (and rightfully so) if he was for the Israelites or for the inhabitants of Jericho. The man responded by saying that he was on neither side but that he was the "commander of the Lord's army." This was intriguing not so much for the statement itself but rather for how Joshua reacted to this news.

For what Joshua did was he knelt before this commander. Obviously, this was very strange. After all, Joshua was the rightful leader of the Israelites. However, Joshua also recognized when he was before someone who was a messenger sent by God Himself, and since Joshua knew and understood that he could not succeed without God's help, it became imperative that Joshua obeyed whatever message this commander was about to send to them.

Incidentally, what this messenger had was a battle plan

of how Jericho and its walls were to be destroyed. The first six days, Joshua and his army were to march around Jericho once. Seven priests were to join the army, and they were to be in front of those carrying the ark of the covenant, while they themselves carried trumpets made from ram's horns. No noise, however, was to be made. On the seventh day, Joshua, the priests, and the Israelite army were to march around Jericho seven times, with the priests blowing on their trumpets along the way. Once the army was done encircling Jericho seven times, the priests were to make a long blast of a noise, and once this happened, the Israelite army was to give as loud a shout as possible. If they did all of this, the Walls of Jericho were to come crumbling down. Anyone who survived the walls coming down was to be slaughtered inside. Well, as it turned out, that was almost everyone.

Joshua then gave these instructions to his soldiers and priests. For six days, they marched around Jericho once, without noise or pomp, and on the seventh day they marched around Jericho seven times, and the priests, this time, were blowing on their trumpets. One long blast of the trumpet later, the soldiers made a great noise, and this noise caused Jericho's walls to collapse.

There was one amazing thing, though. Remember Rahab, the prostitute who ensured the safety of the two spies from the king of Jericho? Well, as it turned out, she and her family were the only ones spared from both the crumbling of Jericho's walls and the onslaught brought on by the Israelite army. Just think about that for a second: the person who was the most looked down upon in society was the one who, along with her family, was spared by God's mercy, and it was all because she did something that benefitted God's chosen people Israel. Is that something or what!

This indeed was a tremendous victory for the Israelites, but as great as that moment was, it was what happened afterwards that showed why Joshua was such a great leader. Before the walls of Jericho were destroyed, Joshua and the Israelites made an oath that not only stated that every person other than Rahab and her family were to be killed off but also that there was to be no prize taking. All gold, silver, bronze, and anything else, for that matter, were to be used only in dedication to the Lord.

One man, named Achan, however, disregarded this oath and took some of the metals for himself. What were the consequences of this? Well, the next battle, against the people of Ai (which, by the way, does not mean Artificial Intelligence, and yes, I do not know why some town's name only had vowels in it), ended up being a mitigated and, thankfully, short-lived disaster—this, in spite of the fact that the people of Ai were nowhere near as formidable as the people of Jericho. So Joshua had a decision to make: either to press forwards in the conquest of the promised land or to give up and turn back. What did Joshua do? He first did the right thing by asking the Lord what had happened. Why did the Israelites suffer this failure to an inferior army, right after defeating one of the more formidable ones in Jericho? In other words, as great of a position Joshua had, even he humbled himself before the Lord.

God told Joshua in response that someone had disobeyed orders. They took some things that were supposed to be dedicated to the Lord when they were not supposed to after God delivered Jericho into the hands of the Israelites. Whoever did this had to be destroyed, and this had to be done because until that person was punished, Israel could not defeat its enemies and survive, since it would no longer have God by its side. The following day, Joshua and all the Israelites in Canaan presented themselves before the Lord to see who was the scourge of Israel that caused the defeat and remove them. The numbers were reduced, first by the name of the tribe to which that person belonged, then by clans and families, until finally, it was revealed to be Achan: yes, the same one who did the dirty deed of taking things that belonged to God Himself.

Why the Lord did not reveal this to Joshua sooner is a mystery. Maybe it was because God wanted to test Joshua, to see if he would do what was necessary before the next battle. Or perhaps it was because the truth had to be revealed in a special way, lest Joshua and the people deny this spoken word. Whatever the case, once the lot of blame fell to Achan, he did confess to what he did, and sure enough, both he and his children and property were destroyed, since they broke the 10th commandment: "Thou shalt not covet" (Exodus 20:17).

Now, the Israelites were ready for battle, and in the subsequent rematch against the armies of Ai, they soundly defeated them. Other events took place while Joshua was Israel's first judge, such as the Gibeonites making a treaty with Israel through deception. Why did they do this? Because the Gibeonites had every reason to fear that the Israelites would destroy them if they did not make a treaty with them. As it turned out, the Gibeonites chose the smart route and became useful for Israelite purposes for a long time.

Another event that took place was when those dreaded Amorites were destroyed in a battle where God kept the sun up so that Joshua and his army could finish the task that they started. Joshua made this petition to God because he had reason to believe that the Amorites might have time to regroup and escape in the middle of the night if the daytime did not last just a little bit longer.

Also, some of the first territories of the Israelites were divided up, and among those to make his claim was Caleb, the same one who gave a positive report of the land of Canaan. It is amazing to know that even at eighty-five years of age, Caleb was still willing and able to fight for his portion of the promised land. It was a credit to this man, and an example for the elderly today, that you are never too old to make a contribution to society.

As for Joshua, his story is just one that I enjoy reading, because he wasn't extraordinary in a human sense, but he was a hero to Israel and to their faith. The best part was that he did not do anything that he wasn't capable of. He was just a man who used the talents and calling that God gave him and took them to amazing heights. Just like Joshua, we too can be great soldiers in the Lord's army, although our weapons are the Bible and its spiritual truth, instead of clubs and spears, and like Joshua, we will have our tests, like his response in the handling of Jericho and the people of Ai. But if we stay in faith like Joshua, we will be able to stand strong in the face of adversity.

Chapter 6
Kings, not Judges
(1 Samuel, chs. 1–15)

Joshua did many wonderful deeds as Israel's first judge, but even he had to die at some point, thanks to what Adam and Eve did in the garden, and so he did, but at a good old ripe age of 110. Afterwards, Israel went through a time of instability. It wasn't like Israel never could find a strong leader after Joshua. Gideon, for instance, won many a battle once he received a series of signs to let him know that he was to lead the Israelites into battle and freedom from the oppressive hand of the Midianites, in spite of the facts that he was the lowest member of his family and tribe and that his clan was among the least in the tribe of Manasseh.

Another fine judge and character, even though he is not widely known, was Jephthah, and his battles against the Ammonites are well chronicled. Of course, probably the most famous of the judges was Samson, whose superhuman strength was one nobody could match but was squandered away with his relationship with Philistine Delilah and the secret to his strength that he told herEventually, Samson did redeem himself in a final act of heroism against the Philistines.

The knock on the Israelites was that once they lost a strong leader, instead of continuing on the path that brought them success, they turned right back to the practices of those that they were supposed to destroy. Yes, they were at least capable of achieving significant military victories. However, they always seemed to forget where their source of strength came from, and that was the Lord Almighty. Without a god-fearing individual to lead them, the Israelites seemed to always stumble and fall, and instead they worshipped other gods. You know how that saying goes, that sometimes people tend to do things the wrong way, instead of doing the things that brought them to a position to succeed. It is like a boxer in the ring who does something else and swings wildly, when it is usually the disciplined and controlled punches that bring him success. Eventually, once the Israelites turned away from the One who gave them strength and victory, they became slaves to one of the peoples that they were supposed to conquer, and they only then would then ask for God's help when they reached rock bottom.

However, it wasn't until 1 Samuel that things got really heated. At the start of 1 Samuel, the acting high priest was a man named Eli. For the most part, Eli did seem to be a decent guy and was fairly effective at his job. However, Eli did have two main flaws. The first flaw was pretty obvious in his reaction to what a woman named Hannah was doing at one of the places of worship. Hannah, you see, was very distressed because she was barren and could not produce any children, which, as you know already, was considered a disgrace during ancient times. So Hannah prayed about this, but Eli took a look at her and noticed that only her lips were moving; she was not actually making any sounds when she prayed, so Eli assumed that Hannah must be drunk; how else to explain her behavior? In reality, however, Hannah was merely praying through her heart, which, by the way, is how you are supposed to pray, with or without actually speaking. So, it is fair to say that Eli's first flaw was that he was too judgmental.

The second flaw might not have been so obvious, but it did deal with Eli's handling over the improper conduct of his sons. You see, Eli's sons were known for treating the Lord's offering with absolute contempt. Instead of accepting boiled meat and giving it to the Lord as a sacrifice, which was what they were supposed to do, as sons of the high priest, they would accept raw, uncooked meat and then proceed to eat it for themselves. This was bad enough. What made things even worse, however, was that they also would sleep with the women who were at the temple of meeting, who were only there, probably, to provide some menial task for the priests, such as cooking and cleaning for them. In the process, Eli's sons corrupted the women as well.

Eli at first seemed to do the right thing and rebuked them for their mistakes. However, Eli's sons would continue to do their abominable practices, and this became a huge problem, especially when Eli did nothing about it. This was the same mistake so many churches make today; they see that a pastor who, by the way, is most likely beloved by the community, but when that pastor or, for that matter, someone in the congregation, commits a terrible sin, mostly likely adultery with someone he or she is not married to, but it could be something else, nobody is there to correct that person's behavior and ask for a change in conduct. Yes, as a Christian, you are supposed to forgive a neighbor of their sins. However, where many people get it wrong, and Eli in this case made this flub, is that just because you forgive another person of transgressions does not mean that you no longer discipline them. What Eli should have done was remove his sons in their role as priests, but by allowing them to keep their positions, Eli was telling his sons that even though what they did was wrong, it would still end up being okay and he would not do anything about this situation. As high priest, Eli failed in this role as the Israelite spiritual leader.

There were two prophecies concerning what was to happen to Eli and his sons for the atrocities that the sons committed, as well as Eli's failure to correct them. The second one, with a little boy named Samuel hearing the Lord's calling him into service, we will get to shortly.

Before that, however, it is important to mention a few things about the first prophecy.

First, there was a description of Eli's family history. The man of God, who went to Eli so that the Lord asked him why, if the Lord gave Eli and his family the honor of being the Lord's priests, had Eli favored his sons over worship and sacrifices to the Lord, and not only that, but had the honor of wearing an ephod in the Lord's presence? This is extremely significant, especially when you look into Exodus 28. An ephod, you see, is a breastplate that was made during the time Israel was in the wilderness, and it was only to be worn by Aaron and his descendants. So not only was Eli a Levite, but it also meant that he and his family were direct descendants of Aaron.

Second, if you look up Exodus 29:9, you will see that the Lord promised Aaron and his sons that they would always receive the priesthood. However, by Hophni and Phinehas, who were Eli's sons, committing the abominations that they did before the Lord, and Eli not rectifying the situation and removing his sons from the priesthood, Eli's family was now to be excluded from those responsibilities, and their lives were to be cut short in their primes. Yes, a descendant of Aaron's could still be a high priest, but now it would have to be someone who is either a cousin or uncle, or even a nephew, of Eli's, and not any of his sons.

Lastly, it was revealed that Hophni and Phinehas would both die on the same day and be replaced by a faithful priest. This role of faithful priest was initially fulfilled by Zadok, who served loyally under King David, and later on Solomon. Eventually, things would be so bad for Eli's descendants that they would be begging for a priestly office of some kind, not for prestige but rather to survive starvation.

Now, onto that little boy named Samuel. Remember that lady named Hannah? Yeah, you know, the one who was barren and whose prayer was misinterpreted by Eli as the rambling on of a drunkard? Turns out her prayers for a child were answered and that she had a kid named, of course, Samuel. Furthermore, Hannah made a promise, which she did fulfill, that she would give up Samuel into the house, or tent, of the Lord. Little did Hannah know how significant this decision to give up her son to the priesthood would become.

Anyway, Samuel eventually was growing up, as boys and girls do, and was almost considered to be a young man by the standards of Jewish tradition. One night, however, Samuel's sleep was disturbed by someone calling him. The voice seemed so natural, in fact, that Samuel makes the mistake of believing that it was Eli calling him, when in fact he did not. This routine happened three times, and on the third time, Eli finally discerned for Samuel that it might be God Himself calling Samuel, so he told Samuel that if the voice called him again, to say, "Speak, Lord, for your servant is listening." Interestingly, in 1 Samuel 3:1, it was mentioned that God's word was rarely revealed in those days, and not many saw visions. Basically, you either had a lot of deists, who knew God existed but did not believe that He controled the affairs of the world, or you had a lot of people who said they obeyed the Lord but did not put His words into practice.

So, the Lord called Samuel one more time, and Samuel said exactly what Eli suggested to him, and God revealed everything to Samuel that was spoken to Eli concerning him and his family and how they were to come to pass. This was a frightening and terrible thing to hear for poor Samuel, and it was so for two reasons. First, because Eli was Samuel's mentor, and as someone Samuel looked up to, it was hard for Samuel to believe that this man, who not only was the equivalent of Samuel's big buddy but also was this great high priest, could do anything wrong, especially in terms of covering for the sins of someone who sinned exceedingly against God, yet it sounds like that was exactly what Eli was doing (it was).

The second reason why Samuel did not want to hear this was because of what might happen to him should Eli find out what the Lord spoke to him. Such a message of telling Eli that he and his sons would die for the sins they committed could result in being ridiculed, at best, and at worst, result in Samuel being either excommunicated from the Jewish faith, which basically meant being a man without a country, or executed for what Eli might interpret to be blasphemy. Eli, however, wanted to know what the Lord said to Samuel on that night and even went so far as to say that if Samuel did not reveal this information to Eli that the Lord would punish Samuel severely for not revealing His word. Samuel was petrified, I am sure, yet he did not hide any specifics from Eli as to what was to happen. Normally, such news would initially bring on a disbelief from the party receiving such news, followed up by intense anger, but to Eli's credit, he instead stated that God's decision on Eli's life, as well as the lives of his sons, was just.

The good news is that as Samuel grew up, he not only becomes an effective leader but was also recognized by many to be a prophet sent by God. However, as Wade Barrett from World Wrestling Entertainment would say, "I've got some bad news for ya," and the bad news was that Israel's next battle against the Philistines, who by now had been a thorn in Israel's side for a long time, led into one of the worst days in the history of ancient Israel. First, Israel was losing this battle, so they brought in the ark of the covenant, the same one Joshua and his army used in winning battle after battle, all in hopes of turning the tide of this battle around. The Lord, however, was not with them on this day, probably because Hophni and Phinehas, the two men who were such a disgrace to the Lord's priesthood, were two of the people carrying the ark.

Now, the Philistines knew the power that this ark

possessed, and they had some firsthand experience as to how this ark would bring the Israelites victory when it seemed like they would lose, so the Philistines were understandably afraid of the ark, but only at first. Eventually, however, the Philistines worked up their courage and not only won the battle and killed 30,000 men in the process, but two of the Israelite casualties were Hophni and Phinehas, as they were slaughtered in the heat of the battle. Also, the Philistines somehow managed to get a hold of the ark of the covenant itself.

Shortly afterwards, a messenger came from the battle and told Eli what happened. By this time, Eli was nearing 100 and was blind, so he knew that his time on Earth was drawing to a close. The messenger told Eli that Israel lost the battle, his sons were now dead, and the Philistines now had possession of the ark of the covenant, and it was at the mention of this news, about the ark, that Eli fell from his chair, broke his neck, and died right on the spot.

That very same day, Phinehas's wife was about to give birth to a son. As soon as she heard about what happened to not only her husband but her father-in-law and brother-in-law as well, she was in complete despair, so much so, in fact, that she herself died shortly after giving birth. Israel's glory seemed to have departed, and it could not have happened at a worse time. Yet, it also showed you that none of this would have happened had Hophni and Phinehas not acted in such a condescending manner and had Eli done his job of punishing them for their actions.

However, just when it seemed like the Philistines had achieved total victory, a funny thing happened. You see, the main god of the Philistines was Dagon, and the Philistines didn't see much of a problem with having the ark of the covenant next to a statue of Dagon's image. After all, the ark had proven to be ineffective against their army. Unfortunately for Dagon, the next day his statue was found to have its head severed from its body, where it was laid facedown before the ark of the covenant. At first, the Philistines thought of this as nothing more than a co-incidence, so they put the head of Dagon back to its proper spot. The following day, however, not only was Dagon's head back on the floor but his hands are cut off and on the ground as well. At this, the Philistines knew that they were in deep trouble, not by a human army but by God Himself. It didn't even matter where the Philistines had the ark; whether it was Ashdod or Gath, the results were the same: pestilence upon the Philistines in the form of tumors. By the time that the ark had reached Ekron, it was pretty evident to the Philistine people that their arrogance in their god had cost them big time and that the God of Israel was superior. It just shows you that the Lord is not just some pet that you can control on a Saturday or Sunday; if anything, it is He who is in control of each and every situation.

Samuel eventually became a fully grown and

responsible man, ready to lead Israel into battle against the Philistines as Israel's leader, and also as who would turn out to be its last judge. Once Samuel was ready to lead, the battles against those dreaded Philistines turned to Israel's favor, as the people of Israel were beginning to understand that it was their Lord and God that they should rest their hopes on, and nothing else. All seemed to be good, right? However, Samuel eventually grew old, and knowing this, he tried to appoint his sons Joel and Abijah as judges, which wasn't such a bad idea on paper, since you had to have some sort of leadership once Samuel was gone. The problem with Joel and Abijah, however, was the same one with Hophni and Phinehas years earlier, and that was the fact that they were immensely corrupt. Only, instead of making invalid and disrespectful sacrifices and sleeping with women near the Lord's tent, Joel and Abijah made dishonest gain by taking bribes, which in turn perverted justice that was being carried out. Thus, the elders of Israel confronted Samuel about this, and they asked Samuel to appoint not a judge, but a king, to lead Israel.

Samuel, of course, was displeased with this, because he thought that only God Himself was Israel's true king. Samuel also knew, however, that Eli had made the mistake of not reprimanding his sons and removing them from the priesthood once he found out about their conduct. So Samuel did the smart thing and prayed to God over Israel's current situation, and this would become the reason why Samuel is a highly regarded character in the Bible some 3,000 years after his death.

Basically, the Lord's response to Samuel's prayer was to let the people of Israel have their king, but it was not because the people were rejecting Samuel; rather, the people were once again rejecting their God. Once God gave Samuel the news of what he should do, Samuel told the people of Israel what was to happen when they had their king, which was information that God, of course, already knew. It was now becoming crystal clear that these people in Israel did not want to fight for themselves against an enemy that they needed to defeat; they wanted to be like other nations and have a king do it for them. This was all well and good, except that God should have been considered to be their king and that God was winning battles for them. Yet, did these people give God the rightful glory? No, they did not! They did not see that they already had a heavenly king who provided everything they needed, including total victory from their enemies, and that was why at that time the people of Israel wanted an earthly king.

Samuel went out, albeit in an unhappy mood, to find someone to anoint as Israel's first king, and the Lord led him to a man named Saul, who was from the tribe of Benjamin. At first, this seemed like the perfect choice: Saul stood head and shoulders above the average Israelite in terms of height; he was from the smallest tribe in Israel, so he knew something about humility; and, as it turned out, he was a very courageous and skilled leader in the heat of battle.

However, it wasn't long before the flaws in Saul's character were revealed. Before one of the battles against the Philistines began, the plan was for Saul not only to wait for Samuel to arrive so that Samuel would make sacrifices before the Lord but also to wait on the Lord's instructions. For seven days Saul and his army waited for Samuel to arrive at a place called Gilgal, where the Israelite army was hiding from the vicious attack of the Philistines. Only Samuel did not show up when Saul and his army thought that he should have, and Saul's men were scared to the point where they started to scatter. In reality, they probably got impatient and lost their poise. Saul himself started to worry, probably because he could not see how he would be able to defeat the Philistine army if his entire unit deserted him, so to keep the troops where they were, Saul instead made a sacrifice to God himself, even though that was not what he was supposed to do.

The problem with finishing a sacrifice before Samuel did arrive was that Samuel was still the Lord's prophet, even though he no longer was their judge, and by offering sacrifices to increase his chances against the Philistine army, as opposed to waiting patiently for Samuel to arrive, Saul was rejecting the notion that as Israel's king, his still had to be subjected under the Law and the prophets; thus, he was rejecting the Lord's command. This is why it is not only to do as God says but also to do it in His time, not our own.

Still, Saul had an opportunity to redeem himself. In other words, God was willing to give Saul a second chance. Unfortunately, it was this opportunity of a second chance that Saul would quickly squander. Before a battle against the Amalekites, Saul was instructed to destroy all of the Amalekites: men, women, children, even their animals, were to be destroyed. Nothing was to be spared. Victory was certain, because God was going to punish the Amalekites for waging war against the Israelites instead of helping them once the exodus from Egypt happened. Saul did attack the Amalekites, who were then slaughtered in battle.

However, the Lord's command was that everyone and everything that was or belonged to the Amalekites was to be completely and utterly destroyed. In this case, Saul did not fail to do his job; he disobeyed, which was even worse, in a way. You see, if Saul had merely failed, it would have meant that he gave his all and the results just did not work out for him. In this case, though, he could have destroyed the good cattle and sheep along with the bad, and Saul could have killed Agag, the Amalekite king, but he did not do so. The sheep and cattle were later on used as sacrifices, but these were completely irrelevant, and what Saul did was not approved either by the Lord or by Samuel. More important than sacrifice was doing what the Lord commanded, and that was something Saul was not doing.

The worst part, though, was that later on, Saul made a monument dedicated to himself. Well, that was the final straw! Saul was now not only disobeying God's will and instructions but he was now also making excuses as well, and while Saul was once a humble young man from the tribe of Benjamin, he now was starting to show traits of pride, arrogance, and conceit. As a result, Saul still had the official title of being Israel's king, but he now had lost the backing of the Lord; if Israel won a battle, it would no longer be because of Saul's abilities. Also, while Samuel later on did kill Agag, he was still displeased with the actions of Saul—so much, in fact, that the friendship that they once had and Samuel treasured so much was now completely and irreversibly severed. A new king had to be anointed, one that at the time had no relationship with either Samuel nor Saul, but little did either man know at the time that the one to be anointed was the least likely person of all. It was this person, who was only a little boy at the time, who would not only be the next king of Israel but also the driving force behind what would become the golden age of ancient Israel. Yes, I am talking about that certain someone named David.

Chapter 7
King after God's Heart (Book of Ruth; 1 Samuel 16; 2 Samuel 24)

To begin this chapter, one must go backwards in the Bible, to the book of Ruth. At that point in time, the judges were the ones ruling Israel, and it would continue until Israel's last judge, Samuel, anointed Israel's first king, Saul. There was a woman named Naomi at this time, who originally was from a little town called Ephrath, which later became famously known as Bethlehem. She moved to some land in Moab, and as we said in chapter 3, and as anybody who reads the Bible would know, the people of Moab were descendants of Lot. Naomi had a husband who accompanied her, and they had two sons whom they brought with them, Mahlon and Killon. The husband of Naomi died later on, but the two sons eventually married two women who happened to be Moabites, one named Orpah and the other one named Ruth.

Here was the ironic thing, though; as people from the southern portion of Israel, the residents of Ephrath knew the hostilities that they had against the people of

Moab. Both clans were descendants of Abraham, but that did not matter, because the Israelites and Moabites hated each other terribly; the people of Moab didn't like the fact that the Israelites were pillaging their towns, while the people of Israel did not like how the Moabites were trying to lead them astray by serving other gods, which would result in the curse of the Almighty God upon them. The Hebrew people did not necessarily prohibit a marriage between an Israelite and someone who was a Moabite; however, by denying those who did a place in the assembly of the Lord, the Israelites made it clear that to marry a Moabite meant to be cut off from his or her own people. Needless to say, the decision of the two sons of Naomi to marry Moabite women was more than just a little bit of a head scratcher.

After a time, though, Naomi's two sons died, and they left their wives without any children, which, as we know, in ancient times was translated as being disgraced or cursed. By this time, the famine that led Naomi and her family to Moab was over, and since this land that Naomi had lived in for a long time had given her nothing but grief and sorrow, due to the loss of her husbands and sons, she set back to the land that was under the tribe of Judah. Orpah and Ruth wanted to stay with Naomi; after all, Naomi was nothing but kind and considerate towards them, and they shared in the grief that Naomi had, especially in their husbands. Naomi, however, would not allow this. At that point in time, it seemed like the pathway for Naomi now was nothing but desolation and grief, with a sense of hopelessness. Figuring that her daughters-in-law were still young and healthy, Naomi did not want to burden them on this trail that she was to take but rather wanted them to move on with their lives, marry others, and have some hope that maybe better days were around the corner.

Looking at the scriptures through modern eyes, I am fairly certain that many people today would admire Orpah and her decision to leave Naomi more than the choice that Ruth made. I mean, yes, I am sure that leaving Naomi to fend for herself after the loss of Orpah's husband and Naomi's son was painful, but many would applaud Orpah for moving on and going on a different path to see what possibilities laid on the horizon. There are those who would even wish that they had the courage to take the risk of traveling into the unknown.

However, as people in the modern age would applaud Orpah's decision to leave her mother-in-law Naomi, let us also applaud Ruth's decision to stay with Naomi. In a self-seeking, me-first world, Ruth showed a loyalty and love that is very rare in this day in age. In today's world, we just do not have the patience and love to make marriages work; everything is more about what is convenient for that person. If that were not the case, we would not have so many marriages end up in divorce, and both the husband and wife suing each other for the most minor of disagreements and frivolous manners. Also, if you notice the culture in Hollywood today, you see how most of the mothers-in-law and fathers-in-law in those movies are an absolute dread to deal with. If I didn't know any better, I would say that in the eyes of the Hollywood elite, Ruth's decision to stay with Naomi all the way to Judah would be seen as unrealistic.

However, in the end, Ruth did stick it out with Naomi on the journey, and as it turned out, it was the best choice she made in her life. One day, Ruth decided to work on one of the harvest fields in hopes of providing for both her and Naomi. This was a risky adventure for Ruth, since she was still a young woman, and, I am sure, very attractive. For what Ruth was doing was working alongside men, and it would have been easy, or at least tempting, for these men to have taken advantage of her without anyone noticing.

Well, it just so happened that one of Naomi's relatives, a man named Boaz, was the owner of the very field that Ruth was working on, and as he was returning from a business trip in Bethlehem, he noticed Ruth working in the fields. So Boaz asked one of his hired hands to inquire about Ruth's identity, and once he found out that she is staying with Naomi and helping out, Boaz told Ruth to no longer work with the men in the harvest fields; instead, Boaz had her stay with the servant girls, which was significant because the servant girls were the ones who bound the grains into sheaves after the men were done harvesting the grain out of the ground. Had Ruth gleaned the leftovers while the men were still working, there was a high risk of a man raping her without anybody being the wiser, and there could have been what we today would call a work-related accident, as well. However, by having Ruth wait until the servant girls bound the sheaves to glean over the fields, Boaz was saving her from any sort of injury, physical or otherwise.

Well, when Ruth got back home to tell Naomi of what had happened, and also who took notice of her, the first thought, paradoxically, that Naomi had, was to get Ruth ready for date night. Because let's face it: women gleaning over some field turned rich, Israelite land owners on! What Naomi was especially happy about was that it was Boaz who took notice of Ruth, since it was the responsibility of the nearest of kin of the widow's husband to take care of the widow once the husband died, back in ancient times. Plus, Naomi knew Boaz enough to believe that he was a man of high character. Now, as it did turn out, there was somebody more closely related to Ruth's now deceased husband than Boaz, but after he realized that he had to marry Ruth, the man exercised his right to not redeem Naomi's property, and I am certain it was because Ruth was a Moabite. Well, it just so happened that the person next in line after the guy who turned Ruth down was Boaz, and Boaz was more than happy to redeem Naomi's estate, as was the custom in ancient Israel, and it wasn't too long before he and Ruth got married.

Why is this story mentioned at all? After all, without any more facts, one might say that this seemed to be nothing more than a cute love story. The reason is written in Ruth 4:21–22, and it stated that through Ruth and Boaz, they became the parents of Obed, who in turn was the father of Jesse, and it was on Jesse's property that Samuel was to find out whom he was to anoint as Israel's next king once Saul had abandoned God's principles and message for his very own.

So Samuel set out on his way to anoint God's next chosen one, the next king. However, Samuel had to do this in secret; since Saul technically still had the official title as king of Israel, he had already known in advance that someone was going to replace him on the throne and that someone was not going to be one of his sons, since he disobeyed God's command. Samuel was very concerned about this and thought that Saul would kill him if the king found out about Samuel's true mission. Therefore, Samuel had to make himself as unsuspecting as possible by stating that he was on his way to Bethlehem to make a sacrifice for the Lord, nothing more.

Well, Samuel was telling part of the truth, even going so far as to invite Jesse and his family to this sacrifice. Once the consecration was complete, it was time to decide who would be the next king of Israel. Eliab, being the firstborn, was brought to Samuel first, and initially, Samuel thought that Eliab was the one to be anointed king. This man definitely stood out, Samuel thought, since he had both the stature and the commanding presence akin to that of a ruler.

Well, Eliab may have seemed to have the qualities needed to be a leader in Israel, and he obviously had that perception about him, since he was the firstborn in his family; thus he had to be a leader on certain occasions, but God did not see people the way most people see each other. Man might look at outward appearances, which Eliab had plenty to offer, but God looks to the inwards souls and spirit of man, and based on what God was seeing, there was something inside Eliab's spirit that was lacking. Next up to see if he was king was the next born son, Abinadab, followed by Shammah, but the Lord did not choose these two, nor did He choose the next four sons of Jesse after them. It seemed like nobody who was the son of Jesse was meant to be king.

As it turned out, however, one of Jesse's sons did fail to show up to the meeting, and since he was the youngest son, this young man was busy tending to Jesse's sheep. Until this youngest son arrived, Samuel, Jesse, and all the others had to wait until he showed up. When this youngest son of Jesse finally arrived, the Lord told Samuel in his very being that this boy, who was indeed handsome, with a ruddy complexion, but still nothing more than a young lad, was to be the next king of Israel. So, it was David, the youngest son of Jesse, and the great-grandson of a Moabite woman, who was now to be the one chosen to lead the Israelites as its next king. It just proves that God is the one who can lead the paths of men, and not other people, because if that were not the case, then David, as the runt of Jesse's family, would not be even close to kingly material, certainly not in the eyes of men.

Later on in 1 Samuel 16, we learn a little more about David, as he just so happened to have already been accepted into the services of Saul. By this time, Saul had an evil spirit that constantly was tormenting him, so he needed someone who was skilled as a musician to calm him down and have those evil spirits leave him. Well, it just so happened that in addition to tending his father's sheep, David was also gifted in the playing of the harp, and whenever David played the harp, the evil spirits that would torment Saul would leave, if only temporarily. In addition, David also provided food for the Israelite army like cheese and milk, and he even was appointed to be one of the armor bearers of Saul. Why Saul would give someone like David such a responsibility is a mystery, although David did prove to be loyal in this role, but there were two things that were certain. One, that Saul at the time did not see David as a threat, and for good reason: David was just a little boy who was serving underneath Saul in a couple of minor roles and who also just so happened to be the son of Jesse from Bethlehem. The other certainty, however, was that the fact that David was entrusted to be Saul's armor bearer meant that he had to have been exposed to some sort of military campaign, and it might be this experience that would be the hint as to what happened next.

Here was what went down. The Philistines had a champion among their ranks, a man who was built up as being unbeatable, and for good reason. This man, who was labeled as the best fighter that the Philistines had, was from the town of Gath, and his name was Goliath. Obviously, most anybody knows something about Goliath and his reputation, but for those who do not, here is what made him so tough to defeat. The first thing to notice about Goliath was, obviously, his sheer size. You are talking about a guy who was nine feet tall, which meant that he could make Shaquille O'Neal look like Gary Coleman. Then, you add on to the fact that this giant, this Leviathan, had all sorts of armor all over his body, a huge spear, and a seemingly impregnable shield, and what you are talking about here was a one-man weapon of mass destruction more devastating than a Big Show uppercut. (Yeah, I am a bit of a wrestling fan.)

Well, for 40 straight days, Goliath kept hurling insults at the Israelite army and their God, and he even challenged Saul to find someone to face him in one-on-one combat, and truth be told, who could blame Goliath for feeling so confident? Even in a group effort, the Israelites had trouble handling this guy, so a chance to go one-on-one with this guy was such a terrifying prospect that no prize could possibly be worth it. It even seemed like suicide to try to take Goliath on. One day, however, David was doing his usual chore of supplying the army with food and minding his own business when Goliath hurled his usual insults at the Israelite army, and whereas everybody else looked on with fear and hopelessness, David was nothing if not irate. How dare this foreigner, this pagan, hurl insults on both God and His people! This right here was the type of righteous anger we Christians need to get rid of the evils of this world from our lives and neighborhoods, no matter how great the obstacle.

David then inquired of the prize given to the man who could defeat this Philistine giant, though in reality David most likely would have done it for free. The oldest brother, Eliab, overheard this and tried to reprimand David as merely someone who was bloodthirsty and just enjoyed watching the battles as they take place. In reality, Eliab was not only jealous because his younger brother was showing him up in the courage department but also confused where David was getting this courage from. There also was the factor that Eliab might sincerely care for David, believing that if his younger sibling engaged in a battle against Goliath, David was almost guaranteed to die from it.

Saul overheard what was going on, and when David said that he was willing to fight the giant who had caused so much despair among the Israelite ranks, Saul initially tried to dissuade David from this battle. After all, Goliath was not only a giant but one who was experienced in the ways of war, and as such a man who had been fighting (and a natural at that) since his youth, it looked on paper that he should make quick work on such a young up-start as David. As it turned out, however, what Saul and his men did not know was that David had some experi-ence as well, albeit not in the typical sense of a battle. You see, David in his time as someone who tended his father's sheep had faced two animals, a lion and a bear. In both instances, David not only was successful in fending these animals off of the sheep that they were trying to kill but also killed both the lion and the bear as well. David clearly had the belief that if he could defeat a lion and a bear, he could also take on and defeat Goliath.

Now, the rest of the Hebrew army and Saul still did not believe that David had a prayer in the world against their Philistine foe, although they certainly must have at least admired his courage and faith in God, but Saul at least had David put on Saul's armor. It was possible that Saul and the army commander Abner thought that if David at least had armor on, that might delay the gi-ant Goliath some so that the Israelite army could get in position for a counterattack against the rest of the Philistine army, who would watch the battle casually, since they obviously thought of Goliath as unbeatable. Only problem with Saul's plan was that David could not wear the armor and be effective with it, since he had never worn such a thing in his life. It is kind of hard to defeat someone when you are weighted down so much just from your own equipment! Instead, David found five smooth rocks near a stream, and with a staff and a sling to go along with these stones, David felt ready at last to face, get ready, a nine-foot giant with spears, swords, and javelins, with a shield, armor, and a helmet! This looked like a colossal mismatch.

When Goliath saw that David was Saul's champion to go up against him, Goliath could not believe this! He had to be asking himself, "Are you kidding me, Saul?" It basically was a little boy with primitive weapons going up against not just someone who had what was considered at the time to be modern weaponry but also, as mentioned before, a one-man WMD. Goliath must have thought that this was going to be an easy task, and understandably so, but if that was the case, which I am certain it was, then that was to be his mistake and undoing. Goliath did come in for the attack, but shockingly, so did David. As it turned out, however, this was what David wanted from the onset, so that he could get Goliath in position, and with the firing of one of the stones that David had collected upstream earlier, David somehow connected with the forehead of Goliath, in the one place where his body was not covered with some sort of armor. As trained with the sling as David was, it was most likely that he had a little bit of help from God Himself, since it was rare to have the type of precision that David had in landing that one shot, but whatever the case was, it only took that one shot to the head for Goliath to crumble dead like a ton of bricks.

Needless to say, both sides were shocked to their very cores by such a monumental upset, which, by the way, has to be the biggest upset in any battle or competitive sport in world history. However, where the Philistines were disheartened and crestfallen over the defeat of their champion, the Israelite army was pumped up akin to an NHL team coming back from a 3–0 deficit to win a series, and because of the inspiration that David gave in slaying the Philistine giant, the Hebrew army was able to win a decisive battle on this particular day against the Philistines.

All was looking pretty good for David. He became fast friends with Saul's son Jonathan; he grew into a higher rank in the army, and the people seemed to adore him like the hero that he was. Unfortunately, during this time, some women made a song of praise, where they sang about Saul killing his thousands and David killing his tens of thousands. The problem was not so much the praises themselves; if you had people who were secure in their legacy, such comments would not get under their skin all that much. No, the problem was that now Saul was starting to be jealous of David and also saw him as a threat to his kingdom, and that was the concern Samuel had when he decided to go on a mission to find a new king once Saul disobeyed God's command.

The following day, after all these praises were heaped upon David, Saul threw a javelin at him, and did so twice, hoping to pin David against the wall, but David managed to elude them. This should have told David right then and there that Saul had intentions to kill him, but he did agree to the next mission that Saul sent him on, which was another battle against the Philistines, with the reward being that Saul would give one of his daughters into marriage with David should David succeed. Only thing was, Saul did not do this necessarily because he saw the Philistines as a threat to Israel, even though they were, but because he was hoping that David would die in battle, and if David just so happened to have died in battle, then Saul would have been absolved of any blame. David, however, had the Lord on his side, and on this particular mission he was successful against the Philistines, much to the chagrin of Saul.

There were two ironies about the time when Saul was trying to have David killed. One, that David honestly did not know for certain that Saul was out to kill him until his friend Jonathan made mention of it. Just because

Samuel had anointed David to be king, and just because David did, in fact, kill the Philistine giant Goliath, did not mean that David saw himself as anything more than a shepherd boy who just so happened to have been accepted in the Israelite army, which, by the way, was a credit to how humble David was. The other irony was that if there was anybody who had the right to be resentful and have any sort of animosity towards David, it would have been Jonathan. After all, as the son of Saul, Jonathan would have had the right to believe that when Saul died that he would have inherited the kingdom. Yet, in spite of this supposed inheritance that Jonathan could have had, he still decided to be David's friend and help him escape the wrath of Saul. Even Jonathan, at this point, had come to the full realization that his own father was a fanatic who was obsessed with maintaining a stranglehold of power, to the point where he believed that David was his greatest threat, even if David had done nothing to deserve such a status.

As a banquet one night would prove, Jonathan was right in regards to his father. For it was on that night that Saul lost his temper when Jonathan told him that David could not make it to the banquet due to an annual sacrifice that had to be done in Bethlehem. In other words, it really meant what David and Jonathan had been suspicious of, but did not quite know for sure, and that was that Saul was jealous over the success that David seemed to have enjoyed every time he went into battle, and he was getting more credit for victories won than Saul was.

Other events that followed didn't change the situation any. David was going to and forth from all sorts of different places, and Saul, with his soldiers, would be following the trail closely. At one point, Saul even had the priests of Nob killed because they had harbored David, and they also helped him escape before Saul and his men could arrive. Perhaps another irony might have been that in spite of the fact that David was the number one fugitive in the mind of Saul's, he still was able, in the process, to help aide Hebrew cities that were under siege from the true enemies of Israel, and that was the Philistines. Basically, you had an Israelite king trying to hunt down the one who was anointed to take his place, yet the one who was anointed was still defeating the enemies of Israel for the current king.

There later on was yet another mind-boggling thing that was added to the saga of David versus Saul. You see, while Saul and his men could never actually capture David, David actually had two opportunities to kill Saul. However, in both instances, David decided to not go through with the killing of Saul. At first, this makes no sense, because you would think that the best way to keep someone from chasing after you is to personally make sure that they are dead. That being said, the reason why David did not kill Saul was because David still saw Saul as someone who was anointed to be the king of Israel. In the minds of many, if David had killed Saul, it would have been understandable to think that he did it in self-defense, but in David's mind, even if the killing of Saul was for self-preservation, it was considered to be treason, which was the last thing that David wanted to do.

Around the same time, several other events happen. First, the old sage Samuel died at a ripe age, but the later years of his life were filled with heartache over the poor choices and breakup of the friendship he had with Saul. Later on, David and those following him were sent to protect the property of a man named Nabal, and they did an admirable job of it. Nabal, however, treated David's men with scorn and contempt, and it was at this that David was angry enough that he wanted to take Nabal's life for being so disrespectful. Thankfully, Nabal's wife Abigail interceded and prevented David from making a mistake out of anger, knowing full well what a fool her husband was. Not too long afterwards, the Lord struck Nabal dead, and David later on did marry Abigail, one of what turned out to be several wives that David would have.

Now, on to perhaps the biggest irony of David's life. Even bigger than the ones beforehand. After sparing Saul's life a second time, it became crystal clear to David that Saul, while slowing down every once in a while, was never going to stop trying to hunt David down and kill him. So, David, knowing this, realized that he was in desperate help. What did David do? He hid inside the land of the Philistines, the very same Philistines, by the way, who had been whipped in battle when facing David and his men over and over again, and while I am sure that the Philistines had to have felt a little glad that David was at last on their side, particularly some of their commanders, there also was no way that the Philistines could have possibly trusted David, not with all the embarrassments that he had caused them, plus the rumors that it was David who was to be anointed king of their enemies, the Israelites.

The next few events that would unfold would see to it that David was not to be a part of the next important battle between the Israelite army and the Philistine camp. By this time, Saul was in perpetual fear. He noticed the Philistine army at one of their camps, and based on primary intelligence, the odds of winning this battle were not very good. At first, Saul did actually make an attempt to inquire any words from the Lord. However, by this time, Saul had burned so many bridges with the Lord that he got no response. It didn't help Saul any that the Lord knew full well that Saul was only asking for such a request for himself, and not to glorify God, or that he continued to try to have David executed.

Saul then tried to ask for guidance from a medium. Only thing was, all this was doing was showing how desperate Saul had become, because earlier, Saul had made a ban on those practicing witchcraft and being mediums. This medium was initially afraid for her life upon the request of a certain stranger, since there was such a ruling in Israel. But the stranger (who was really Saul in disguise) assured her safety. When the medium asked Saul who to bring back from the dead, Saul made a request that Samuel be brought back. It was very strange for Saul to ask this because the Lord forbade his people from contacting mediums, and Samuel was a man who served the Lord diligently when he was alive, but Saul figured that maybe Samuel could give him advice one last time before a battle began; albeit this time, it was through the agent of a medium. Samuel, however, was to disappoint Saul with some bad news. This next battle was to result not just in defeat for Israel but also in the death of Saul and his sons. At last, Saul was to pay the ultimate price for disobeying God's command, and that price was to be his life.

Meanwhile, Achish, the commander of the Philistine camp, wanted David to come with him in the next battle against Saul and the Israelites. Unfortunately for David (or maybe he did luck out), most of the soldiers and generals underneath Achish were not exactly thrilled with the thought of David being on their side and in their camp, as they never fully trusted David to begin with. Not wanting any division among the troops before this next big battle was to commence, Achish decided to send David and his men back to their post. What Achish failed to realize was that by doing this, he actually made things easier for David in that David now did not have to fight against Saul, and it was the code of not hurting the king of Israel that David had always sought.

What is funny is that while the Philistines were preparing for battle against Saul and his men, the Amalekites, whom Saul was supposed to utterly destroy but didn't, raided some of the Philistine towns, one of which was a town named Ziklag. The Amalekites killed off the male residents living in Ziklag but took their wives with them alive. Big mistake, because some of the women and children they stole belonged to David and his men. With God giving clearance, and with David and his men motivated with anger and revenge, David wiped out every single one of the Amalekites in sight, other than 400 young men who escaped, and recovered all that was lost.

Now, on to the battle between Saul's men and the Philistines. It was another tragedy for the nation of Israel, as the Philistines brought on a great slaughter. Saul's sons, including Jonathan, who, despite knowing what his father was like stayed with him because Jonathan did love his father, were killed in battle. At some point, Saul realized that he was not going to escape and regroup and, in fact, that the Philistines would not only kill him but humiliate him as well. So he asked his armor bearer to kill him, for Saul was already wounded. The armor bearer, however, balked at such a notion, so Saul decided to then fall on his own sword. The armor bearer, seeing what Saul did, then fell on his sword as well. The Philistines found their bodies the next day; when they came to the now dead body of Saul's, they cut off his head and were about ready to desecrate his body. Thankfully, there were some brave Israelite men who came in the cloak of darkness to get Saul's body out of there so that he could at least get a decent burial.

So, you would think that now with the death of Saul, along with his sons who went into battle with him, that it would clear the path for David to be Israel's king and also cheer him up that he did not have to do anything against Saul and his family, but that they died in battle anyway, right? Not so fast! When David found out about the death of Saul and his sons, and that an Amalekite finished the deed on Saul, for even after Saul falls on his sword, he was still alive, David had the man slaughtered. As for the path to becoming king, David was made king of Judah by some members of his army and resided in Hebron for a time. However, Abner, who, as we have mentioned already, was the commander of Saul's army, took one of Saul's sons who did not participate in the battle against the Philistines, named Ish-Bosheth (why not just name the poor guy Harry?), and made him king of Israel.

Now, I am sure you are wondering why, if Abner was the equivalent of a United States five-star general, was he not part of the battle that killed both Saul and Jonathan, and all I can say is that there were two possibilities. One was that Saul and Abner made a pact to separate, and if something happened to Saul, there would be an heir among Saul's family that could inherit the throne. The problem with this theory is that Saul was most concerned with his own self-preservation, and a smart king who was concerned with self-preservation would have his commanding officer fight the battles for him, although in those times, the king might have been present in battle as a sign that the leader was with his troops.

Another, and more likely, possibility, was that Abner knew that the Israelites had no hope of winning that particular battle and wanted nothing to do with it. Remember, Abner was nothing if not a military genius, but he also was an opportunist. Abner probably knew that if Saul and the sons who usually went into battle with him all perished then Ish-Bosheth would be king, and since Abner perceived Ish-Bosheth to be weaker than Saul ever was, since he was a youth, Abner thought that this was his opportunity at last to be the unofficial power behind the throne.

Abner, however, made the mistake of not listening to the people of Israel. For if he did, he would have known that most of the people in the land were more in favor of having David be their king. When you had two power-hungry men like Abner and Ish-Bosheth, though, who did not heed what the people wanted, and you had an era when absolute rule by one person was common, you were going to have problems. At last, the manner was settled the only way it could be, and that was through a civil war. David and his men did wind up winning this war, but in a sad turn of events, it also resulted in the deaths of Abner and Ish-Bosheth. You see, in one of the battles, Abner was retreating because David's men were winning the fight. Only problem was that a man named Asahel kept chasing after him. Abner did not want to fight Asahel because Asahel was the brother of Joab, who was commander of David's army at the time, and Abner knew the type of skillful fighter Joab was; the last thing Abner needed was for Joab to have any animosity towards him. Unfortunately, Asahel did not retreat but kept going after Abner, thinking that his quickness would help him. Abner, however, was by far the more experienced fighter, having seen men of all shapes and sizes come and go; thus, he killed Asahel but in self-defense. Joab, and another brother, Abishai, went after Abner for what he did, but before they could get to Abner, some of the Benjaminites, who were still loyal to Saul's family, regrouped and temporarily stopped their offensive.

Later on, at some point in this civil war between David and his men against Ish-Bosheth and his men, Ish-Bosheth started to suspect that Abner might just be conspiring against him. In fact, Ish-Bosheth even went so far as to say that Abner was sleeping with one of the concubines of Saul. Abner was so upset over such an accusation, because even though he was an opportunist, he also did have his standards, and sleeping with one of the concubines of a former king was not something he was willing to do, nor was it necessary for him to do it in the first place, and it was because of this accusation that Abner tried to defect to David's side, and also because of the death of Ish-Bosheth, because without Abner by his side, there was no one who could protect Ish-Bosheth from two raiders who wound up killing him, thinking that they would be in the good graces of David (they ended up dead anyway, because David made a pact with Jonathan years earlier to treat any remaining descendants of Saul and Jonathan with kindness, and since these raiders had killed one of Saul's sons, David wanted to absolve himself of Ish-Bosheth's blood).

In trying to join David's side, however, Abner forgot one important thing: Joab was still part of David's army and still the commander of it, as well. Joab then went ahead and killed Abner in a treacherous manner, partly because he suspected that Abner was plotting against now King David, partly because he did not want to lose his position in the army to Abner, and partly to avenge the death of his brother at Abner's hand. David, upon finding this out, refused to take blame for the death of Abner, and rightfully so, but by the same token, David also knew that Joab was not afraid of overstepping his bounds, and as a result, and as time would prove, while Joab was a great warrior in his own right, David could never let him in his innermost circle. You see, it was not that David did not respect Joab's skills as a soldier of war; he had immense respect for that. But when you have someone who routinely disobeys the command of a political leader, you cannot trust that person at all, and trust is what is needed in order to have the confidence of a king or a president. In a way, the situation between Joab and David is very similar to what went on in the Korean War between the US president at the time, Harry Truman, and General Douglas MacArthur.

Still, whatever the method was, David was now king of all Israel, and what a great king he was. Military campaign after military campaign ended in success; as the Israelites continued to defeat the Philistines in battle, the Jebusites were routed, which at last gave Israel control of what was now their most treasured city, Jerusalem, and the ark of the covenant finally had a resting place, to go along with the permanent kingdom in Jerusalem. At one point, David even was able to show kindness to one of the descendants of Saul, a man named Mephiboseth (again with these confusingly long names), who was a cripple from the time that one of his babysitters tried to run away from the Philistine onslaught when Saul and Jonathan were killed in battle, and she dropped poor Mephiboseth, who was only five at the time, in the process. Other accomplishments included the list of brave things that

David's soldiers did in battle against all sorts of Philistine giants, as is recorded in 2 Samuel 23, because they believed in God and in protecting their king. Also, let us not forget the classical masterpieces that came to be known as the Psalms!

Did David have flaws? Of course he did! Having an affair with Bathsheba while her husband was still alive, and then having that husband killed in battle to conceal the affair, was something that was the type of sleazy behavior that was more expected of Saul than David. I think that it might have been because of this affair that David was a better king and soldier than parent, among other things. For instance, David should have been aware of his son Amnon's feelings towards his half-sister Tamar and corrected this incest type of behavior. Also, when Amnon did rape Tamar, who was the one who took action to discipline Amnon and comfort Tamar? It wasn't David but Tamar's full-blooded brother Absalom. However, where Absalom started to go wrong, and where David should have given him guidance, was that Absalom disciplined Amnon by killing him. A more responsible way to parent someone who was seeking justice was to pay attention to them but teach them that the way to revenge is not through bloodshed but through the trusting and enforcing of laws that discourage possible rapes and murders. What made things even worse, however, was because of the relationship between David and Absalom going sour,

Absalom decided not to wait for his father to die but decided to try to take over the kingdom by force, and this resulted in Absalom's death by the hand of Joab, while the would-be king was hung on a tree in the course of a civil war between father and son.

Speaking of Joab, that was another time where he disobeyed the king's command, which was to spare Absalom. It was also obvious that maybe David should have been a little tougher on Joab, because while he was a great soldier, Joab could also be ruthless, to the point of disobeying orders, and such a headstrong person needed to be reined in a little more; otherwise he would be more of a liability than an asset. This was one situation that David failed in as a military king, because by not disciplining Joab as much as he should have, it allowed Joab to think that he could run free without any consequences.

That being said, what made David such a great king, which is so hard for today's leaders to do, was that he was willing to admit to any wrongdoings and faults that he may have had and try to do better next time. Perhaps it is this ability to be honest with himself as well as humble and having humility that made David the gold standard that all leaders should follow, even to this day.

Chapter 8
The Lord's Prophet
(1 Kings 17–19, 2 Kings 2)

David did have a son who took over the kingdom, by the name of Solomon. Solomon was one of the more memorable kings in Israel's history, as mentioned in the first 11 chapters of 1 Kings, and the reason why he was memorable was because Solomon was labeled as the wisest king in all of history and had riches beyond comprehension. He even had a temple constructed that was dedicated to the Lord, so that it could hold the ark of the covenant, the same project David wanted to build but couldn't because he was a king of war. Eventually, though, Solomon lost his way and forgot what put him in a position of prestige by worshipping false idols, a practice that David would have loathed. It also did not help that it was mentioned in 1 Kings 11:3 that Solomon had 700 wives and 300 concubines (which certainly makes me think that for someone who was supposed to be as wise as Solomon was, this was the most foolish thing anybody could have done, to marry that many women), some of whom must have had some sort of influence on him.

What really hurt Solomon's kingdom, however, was how he treated his workers, in particular those who were not from the tribe of Judah. In addition to his idolatry, Solomon was known for being very hard on his laborers, especially when it concerned the building of the city of Jerusalem. However, if Solomon was harsh on his workers, after his death, Solomon's son Rehoboam thought it would be wise to make the loads on the workers even heavier. Instead, the rest of Israel had enough and rebelled, and the kingdom was split in two. Judah, and later on, the tribe of Benjamin, was still ruled by Rehoboam, but the other 10 tribes in Israel had a king who was not a descendant of David named Jeroboam, who disagreed with how Solomon had earlier overworked the laborers on his pet projects.

At this point, though, it did not matter, since both sides wound up with having their fill of corrupt kings. It got to the point where the people started cursing the fact that they even had a kingdom to begin with, much less two of them, and more often than not the kingdom of Israel and the kingdom of Judah were at each other's throats. Fortunately, when all seemed lost, there came upon the scene a prophet in the land who was focused more on serving God than in serving his own interest, and this is where our next story takes us.

A Tishbite (which seemed to be someone from an obscure location) named Elijah first appeared in 1 Kings 17, during the reign of one of the most corrupt and evil kings in the history of Israel, Ahab. It was bad enough that Ahab worshipped the false idol Baal, which was something that God, of course, would forbid. But Ahab compounded this with the building of Asherah poles and other items used in the idol making of Baal, all in a temple in Samaria. It also did not help that Ahab's wife was an evil woman named Jezebel, who always seemed to push her husband into doing evil the few times he started to develop some sort of conscience.

Well, the Lord had just about had enough of all the corruption that was taking place among His own people, and so, He sent Elijah to tell Ahab that because of his great sins, rain would cease to fall upon his kingdom except by the Lord's word. Elijah also was told to move east of the Jordan River, at the Kerith Ravine, where he was told to drink from the brook there, and the ravens sent by God would provide the food needed to nourish Elijah.

Interesting, isn't it, that in the story of Noah's flood in Genesis, Noah used a raven at one point to try to see if there was any dry land, but the raven never returned to Noah. In this case, however, Elijah's very livelihood and nourishment relied upon a raven finding food and giving the food to him. It was an example of how even ravens are bound to the word of God, and just like Elijah, this raven seemed to acknowledge that to obey God was better than to fly away just on your own free will anytime you pleased.

However, if the Lord was providing food and water to Elijah and, I am sure, the raven as well, He was also sending the worst drought in the history of Israel upon those who were disobeying his command. In the place where Elijah was staying, however, even that region was not getting any rain, and when it dried up, Elijah had to move to a different location. So he packed up and headed down to the house of a widow in a town called Zarephath.

Initially, it looked like God had given Elijah a bad deal. For when Elijah arrived in the town of Zarephath, and met up with the widow there, she was making enough food so that she and her son would have one last meal before they starved to death, because the oil and flour needed to make those cakes of food were that scarce. Elijah did know the circumstances, but he had great faith that somehow, someway, he was going to be provided for. So, Elijah had the widow continue to bake her meal, but he made the request that the first piece should go to him. The widow must have thought that such a notion was the height of insanity! Here she was, along with her son, and they were starving to death, yet she was somehow to provide for this stranger who just came into her house and who claimed to be a prophet from the Lord. Not only that, but this man even made the claim that if the woman provided him food first that they would all of a sudden receive an abundance of flour and oil until the drought ended and rain came falling upon the land. Yet, to the woman's credit, she did as Elijah said, and her faith was rewarded with an abundance of oil and flour, enough, in fact, to last her and her son for a long time.

Sometime later on, however, something terrible happened. The widow's son started to become ill, and he gradually got worse and worse, until finally he died. This makes no sense to either the widow or Elijah, although the widow initially thought that Elijah, through God, was there to remind her of some sin that she had committed. Still, it seemed to make no sense as to why, if God had rewarded the woman's faith in Him and His prophet Elijah in the form of providing food for her and her son until the drought ended, would He then all of a sudden take the widow's son from her.

In my opinion, this was just a test of faith for Elijah and the widow, and the reason why I believe this is because of what happened next. Instead of groveling over the death of the boy, Elijah started to believe that God could restore the boy back to life. In fact, Elijah did not stop asking God to bring life back into the lad, not even after it appeared that nothing happened after Elijah makes his first petition. Elijah continued to make this request to God three times, until, at last, after the third time, the boy's life was restored, and it was this miracle, the first time the Bible recorded someone being raised from the dead, that convinced the widow, beyond the shadow of a doubt, that Elijah was who he claimed to be, and that was a prophet who was sent by God.

Eventually, Elijah got word that, at last, rain was to fall upon Israel when Elijah presented himself before his arch-enemy, King Ahab. Before this happened, though, Ahab asked a man named Obadiah to go through all of Ahab's kingdom in order to find fresh water, in order that they may preserve their livestock. What Ahab did not know, however, was that Obadiah was, in fact, helping those who were on the Lord's side, and even found a safe haven for 100 of the Lord's prophets Jezebel had intended to kill. So what a shock it was for Obadiah when he met up with Elijah, and Elijah told Obadiah that Elijah himself would be present before the king.

I am sure that Ahab was pleased when Obadiah told him that Elijah had been found at last. Ahab blamed Elijah for being the man who had caused the drought in all of Israel to begin with, and the severe famine that went along with it, although Elijah correctly pointed out that it was Ahab and Jezebel who made such a thing happen for their disobedience in God and for leading the people of Israel astray. Finally, Elijah issued a challenge. To prove who had the superior God, Elijah was willing to stand alone against some 450 prophets of the false god Baal. Elijah would worship his God, while the false prophets would worship theirs. Each side would have a bull that they could use to sacrifice to their god. The winner would be determined by which side had a fire going for their sacrifice, but there was a catch to this: neither side could light up the sacrifice by themselves. Their god had to do it for them.

The worshippers of Baal went first, and boy, they were putting on quite a show. They were yelling and dancing frantically around their alter, while begging and pleading with Baal to show himself through fire. There was just one problem: the bull on their alter was not burning up. But they continued on, anyway, this time being even more fanatic, and here was Elijah on the other side, calm as a cucumber, as he was egging them on. "You must yell louder! Maybe Baal is on vacation! Maybe you have to do something to get his attention! I mean, surely he is a god, right?" Elijah would continue to get on their case.

What Elijah knew was that by egging the worshippers of Baal on, he was basically encouraging them to do something just to prove a point, and this time, that foolish action was in the form of the Baal priests cutting themselves open before their god. And yet, when all was said and done, even this display of fanatic devotion was not enough to bring fire upon their alter. The big key here was that many of the people of Israel were witnessing what was going on, many of whom were confused as to which god to serve. By seeing what the worshippers of Baal were doing to themselves, and still not being able to get the desired results that they were hoping for, it now convinced these people that the right side to be on was on the side of Elijah.

Elijah then put 12 stones to signify the 12 tribes of Israel around his alter; then he had both the alter and the wood drenched in water to show that there was no trickery involved, since water in those times would have been thought to have been used to either prevent or put out a fire. From there, all Elijah needed was to make a simple, but effective, prayer before the Lord, and God's fire burned upon Elijah's alter. Elijah proved that he was the one who was worshipping the one true God, and he later on had the worshippers of Baal slaughtered for their sins.

This should have been a great and resounding victory for Elijah, but he could not savor it. Ahab should have at least been happy that rain was finally going to fall upon his land, but instead he reported to his wife begrudgingly that Elijah's God not only made fools of those who worshipped Baal but also killed them. And boy, was Jezebel irate or what! Jezebel was so angry, in fact, that she even stated that she was willing to die if the result was that Elijah was dead as well.

One thing that I do find puzzling is that in spite of his great triumph over Baal's prophets, Elijah was still terrified as to what this woman Jezebel might do to him! Granted, the fact that the prophets of Baal dying did nothing to faze Jezebel might have been part of it, and it seemed like she had some sort of fanatical faith in Baal herself. However, it did not explain why Elijah all of a sudden ran away, even though he had some leverage with his victory earlier. The only thing I can think of, and this is a stretch, is that maybe Elijah felt alone in his principles, that he was the only one worshipping God with a pure heart, while the rest of the people were either led astray or devoted worshippers of Baal. Even then, however, he still had others by his side, and even if that were not the case, the fact that the Lord had always provided for him up to this point should have given Elijah enough insurance to know that he was following the right path, and with that insurance, the courage to face those who were doing otherwise.

Anyway, Elijah did run away, but an angel of the Lord was there to provide food for him, so that he could make it to Mount Horeb. Once there, Elijah stated his case before the Lord that despite his great zeal for God, Elijah had witnessed that all of Israel had seemed to break God's covenant, tear down His alters, and kill his prophets. Just then, a great wind tore into the very mountain Elijah was standing upon, which was followed by a great fire and an earthquake, but the Lord did not show himself through any of these things, but rather, the voice of God came in the form of a still, small voice. It is important that we pay close attention to God's word, for many times, when He speaks to us, it is through what may at the time be something so simple, like the dew of rain or the shape of a cloud, among other signs.

After Elijah repeated his petition to God, he was given a very important message, one that would have a significant impact on the regions in and around Israel for the next generation. First, Elijah was to go back to Damascus, and when he got there, he was to anoint three people. A man named Hazael was to be king of Israel's enemies in Aram; Jehu, who at the time was a commanding officer for Ahab, was to be anointed king of Israel; and Elisha, who wasn't all that well known at the time, was to be the successor of Elijah as the Lord's prophet. Another thing that was mentioned to Elijah, which gave him some comfort, was that the Lord had actually set aside 7,000 others who did not worship any god other that the great Jehovah and made sure that they were spared from the wrath of Ahab and Jezebel.

As events would turn out, these three men, Hazael, Jehu, and Elisha, would become important instruments in God's plan to eradicate Ahab and his followers. Hazael would end up having his fair share of victories over those who worshipped Baal in Israel; Jehu would cleanse Israel of worshipping the false god, including having Jezebel tossed out of a window, only to fall astray later on, once he became king; and Elisha was especially important, giving those who believed in God hope they desperately needed, and also was instrumental in the deliverance of the Israelites from Aramean hands. It was also Elisha who continued the practices of Elijah in terms of preaching about the reformation that the Israelites needed in their spirits.

Perhaps what is most interesting about Elisha, however, was not what he did but what he witnessed that came to pass. For this was one of the great events in biblical history, and Elisha had the honor of being the only primary witness to it. As everyone knows, at some point we will all die, because of the sin that Adam and Eve committed in the Garden of Eden. However, Elijah wound up being an exception to this. Instead of tasting death, like all normal human beings do, Elijah was taken up into the heavens on a chariot, and it was because of Elisha witnessing this event that he is accredited with both prophecy and the ability to perform miracles. In Revelation 11, it was revealed that Elijah would be one of two witnesses that would appear during the time of tribulation, where, yes, he would die at the hand of the Antichrist, but before that happened, he would once again lead people, especially in Israel, into a closer worship with God. Truly, just as Moses was the standard bearer of the law, and David was the golden standard by which all earthly kings must be measured by, Elijah was the prophet of highest quality, one who would pave the way for those after him, like Isaiah, Jeremiah, and yes, his apprentice, Elisha.

Chapter 9
For the Ladies
(Book of Esther)

So far, we have looked into the stories of some of the greatest characters in the Bible. From Noah's faith preceding the Great Flood, to Abraham's belief that he would have descendants represent many nations in spite of his age and Sarah being barren; from Moses leading the Israelites out of the bondage in Egypt, to both Joshua and David showing their true leadership qualities; and from Samuel following God's orders when others had failed him, to Elijah being the standard by which all other prophets were measured, the Bible is vast in its resources when it comes to those who choose God's path instead of taking the easy way out. However, if you notice, most of the people mentioned thus far in this book were men, and what women were mentioned, with possibly the exception of Eve, played something of secondary roles in the stories that this book has up to this page covered. Well, what type of man would I be if I did not make mention of the impact that this one lady had on the history of the Jewish people? Yes, the main character for this chapter is, believe it or not, a woman, and for truly feminine women out there in the world, this one is for you!

To begin this story, let's go back to how the heroine of this story, a woman many in the world know today as Esther, came into such a prominent role in the first place. It was a time of celebration for the people of Persia, as their king, Xerxes, was ruler of a vast empire. To celebrate, Xerxes threw a seven-day party where everyone could get as gloriously drunk as they liked. Xerxes had a beautiful wife named Vashti, who herself threw a party for both her and her friends. At first, there seemed to be no problem with this. However, on the seventh day of festivities, Xerxes decided it was a good time to display Vashti before his guests, and Xerxes, of course, had the typical male ego to do this, as Vashti was a very attractive woman. I mean, let's face it; if a guy is hooked up with a good-looking woman, chances are good that he will brag about it, especially if he has a little too much to drink. Call it a birth defect if you like.

Only one problem: Vashti realized this idea that her husband had, that she was to be made a spectacle of in front of his guests, so she flat-out refused to come to her husband's party. When Xerxes found out about this, he was furious, and after consulting with his advisors, decided to remove Vashti from her position as queen and sent her into exile. Considering how men treated women back in those days, that was not the worst thing to do.

It is certainly better than King Henry VIII of England beheading his wives during the 16th century. Whatever the case, Vashti was removed, and Xerxes was now looking for a new queen. Many in today's culture would look at this story and say that they are in full agreement with what Vashti did, because she stood her ground and was not going to allow Xerxes to treat her as an object. Which is fine, except that she was still going to stay in his palace and eat and drink in his house. Standing your ground is one thing, but when you do so and you still are staying in the same place that the person who intended to make a spectacle out of you owns, then you are not standing your ground so much as you are disrespecting your husband, which even today is not right.

Before I go any further with this story, some of you readers are wondering what on earth the Persian Empire has to do with the Bible. Just this: in spite of the warnings of destruction from prophets like Elijah, Isaiah, Jeremiah, and others should Israel and Judah turn from the Lord, both nations were taken over because they refused to heed those warnings. The kingdom of Israel was destroyed by Assyria in 722 BC, and Judah's kingdom came to an end in 586 BC when Babylon destroyed the city of Jerusalem. The now Jewish people stayed in exile until Babylon was conquered by the Persians some 70 years later. At this point in time, the Jewish people did have some freedoms, like the right to worship God and begin construction in

Jerusalem, but they were not yet a separate kingdom but a part of the Persian Empire. Furthermore, not all Jews decided to move to Jerusalem but rather stayed where they were, possibly because they were more comfortable in their current settings. This was to be very crucial in this story.

Now, back to the story of Esther. After Xerxes got over what he saw as disobedience on the part of Vashti, it was agreed that he find a young virgin female from one of his provinces, in order to be queen in place of Vashti. Well, it just so happened that there was a man who not only resided in the Persian capital of Susa but who was also a Jew from the tribe of Benjamin named Mordecai. This Mordecai, as it turned out, adopted his cousin Hadassah, because she was an orphan. Hadassah, however, was a Jewish name, and because Hadassah and Mordecai were both under Persian rule, they had to come up with a "gentile" name to blend in; thus, Hadassah became to be known as Esther.

After Vashti was removed from being queen, Esther and the other virgin women were taken into the king's court, to see who would most please him. They were also put under the care and supervision of a eunuch named Hegai. In order to weed out the pretenders from the contenders, the women were first given a year's worth of cosmetic treatments, not that this was necessarily going to prove who had what it took to be queen, but it was important that whoever the king chose had to be at least somewhat pleasing to his eyes. The good news, and I am sure many women wish that they could have this, was that all of the cosmetics were paid for by the state. Once the cosmetics were through, the women could then take whatever they pleased in terms of jewelry and place it in the king's palace.

Esther, however, was also intelligent in addition to being beautiful, and thus only took what Hegai suggested to her. It also did not hurt, I am certain, that Esther had already earned the favor of Hegai, since in addition to his advice, he also made sure that Esther got the best cosmetic treatments possible. So, when the time came for Esther to meet the king, Xerxes was blown away by her beauty, and also by her intellect; thus, he made her queen.

All of this seems like nothing more than a nice romantic tale, doesn't it? Great, a Jewish orphan hooked up with the king of what was at the time the most powerful nation on Earth, and it happened after the previous queen fell out of the king's favor. By this point, while it is a nice story out of the pages of a Hollywood movie, it doesn't seem like something worthy of being put in the Bible. After all, where was the adversity? Where was the conflict? Well, as events were about to unfold, Esther's importance would be shown not in the title that she had possessed but by the actions that she took while being queen of Persia.

First off, there was the conspiracy planned between two of the officials serving under Xerxes himself, Bigthana and Teresh. Apparently, Xerxes must have done something to make these two men really angry at him. The Bible was not clear about what caused the dispute; maybe Xerxes did not fulfill his promise to give the two of them a promotion. Perhaps there was a heated argument over the direction Xerxes was taking the empire. Another possibility was that maybe Xerxes somehow belittled the two of them, or he did or said something that Bigthana and Teresh took as an insult. It was even possible that the two conspirators might have been jealous of the king. Whatever the case might have been, Bigthana and Teresh made plans, and those plans mainly entailed the assassination of Xerxes.

There was only one problem for these two conspirators, and it was a factor that they did not count on. First off, in no way am I condoning the assassination of a political leader. It doesn't matter if it is Barack Obama or Abraham Lincoln, George W. Bush or Tony Blair; the way to settle a political dispute is to have a proper and efficient discussion of the issues at hand, not through the killing of someone you disagree with. That being said, if you think about achieving your political goals through violence, you must first be able to keep your plot a secret, and that is something that Bigthana and Teresh obviously failed at, for the person who overheard this plot to kill the king was none other than Mordecai. You know what Mordecai was going to do next; he was going to warn Esther about this plot, because in such a heated situation, Esther might end up getting caught in the crossfire, and you know full well that Mordecai was willing to do just about anything to protect his cousin/adopted daughter. Once Esther found out about this, she reported this to Xerxes, since she had his trust and confidence by now, all the while making mention that it was Mordecai who discovered the plot. Once it was discovered that all that Esther and Mordecai had said was proven true, Bigthana and Teresh were hanged for the crime of treason. Esther now had even more capital with Xerxes, and it was this capital that would prove to be very crucial later on.

It was also around this time that there was another person who found favor with the king, only this one was a man by the name of Haman. In fact, Haman's reputation was such that he even rose to the rank of second-in-command, behind only Xerxes himself. What did Haman do to deserve such an honor? Who knows. However, it is mentioned that he was an Agagite, and there is a reason, in my opinion, why this was important.

If one notices the word "Agagite" closely enough, one would notice that there is a name within that word, and that name is Agag. Also, if one goes back to 1 Samuel 15, or to a part in chapter 6 that I discussed earlier, who was Agag the king of? The Amalekites, the same people the

Lord commanded Saul to utterly destroy, a command, as previously mentioned, that Saul disobeyed.

Why is this important? Here is my theory, and it is one that I am sure has some validity to it. In that battle where Saul was to wipe out the Amalekites completely, he did destroy the ones who were in battle against him, but Saul made the mistake of only routing those in battle. Those who were not in battle did not feel such a wrath (and I am sure that the United Nations would feel cozy at such a thought). Later on, as we know, David had his own dealings with the Amalekites just before he was king of Israel. At a certain point, however, the Amalekites figured out that they could never defeat the Israelites through sheer force, so they decided to blend in and use the art of deception, which wasn't a bad idea, since even the Philistines of that time couldn't stand them. A few centuries went by, but some of them never forgot what the Israelites, or now the Jews, did to them when Saul was king. As a result, you now had Haman, who was in a position of power, who was, in fact, an Amalekite in disguise, but to ensure that he appeared to be harmless, since other nations absolutely loathed the Amalekites as well, he called himself an Agagite. So, what was Haman's mission? To kill the *Jewish people* and wipe them off the map, of course.

Even Haman, with all of the hatred that he had for the Jewish people, though, knew that he had to be subtle, since Xerxes and all of Persia would never endorse the thought of genocide unless there was some sort of proof that they were a danger to the Persian Empire. Truth be told, I think Haman might have given himself more time to plot had it not been for one incident.

You see, when Xerxes gave Haman a promotion to be above all other nobles in his court, he also stated that all should give Haman the honor, as if he were the king himself. Well, everyone, including the royal officers, obeyed this command, with one exception. Who was this one exception who did not bow down before Haman? Mordecai. To what race did Mordecai belong to? *The Jewish people, of course*. So, when Haman found out that Mordecai did not bow down to him, he was initially outraged at such conduct. However, once Haman realized that Mordecai was, in fact, a Jew, Haman now saw an opportunity that he had been seeking all along, and thus he believed that he could convince Xerxes that the Jews were a threat to his very kingdom.

However, in telling Xerxes about a threat to his kingdom, Haman curiously did not mention specifically that it was the Jews who actually were a threat; he slyly stated that a certain people who were scattered among the peoples had a different custom from other peoples and that they disobeyed the king. That being said, there was a reason for this deception. Everyone had no doubt that the customs of the Jewish people were different from all others in the Persian Empire, as were their laws. However, one had to also remember that at the time the Persians defeated the Babylonians to become the most powerful empire on Earth, the Jewish people had been removed from their homeland for 70 years. One of the first things the Persians did once they established their position at the top was to allow the Jewish people to return to the homeland of their forefathers. Many of the Jewish people, needless to say, were thrilled about this, because they now had an established place to return to. Because of this hand in courtesy, the Jewish people had no reason to all of a sudden turn on the Persians; thus, the Jews, while having a different set of beliefs from the Persians, were not disobedient to Persia as long as that empire did not make laws that conflicted with the Jewish religion.

A better way to explain this is in the contrasting between how the Persian Empire in that era treated the Jewish people and how the Romans enforced their Pax Romana, or Roman peace. Unquestionably, the Persians wanted their kings to reign supreme, but they only wanted things that way in regards to how their government was run. In other words, they did not interfere with the religious beliefs of others. The Romans, on the other hand, were given credit for establishing the first republic, where there was some sort of checks and balances between executive and legislative branches of government. For all of that, however, they were also known for being cruel and intolerant to the Jewish people, and the reason why the

Romans treated the Jews with such contempt was because the Jewish people worshipped only one god, something that the Romans could not possibly comprehend, nor could they force the Jewish people to stop their religious practices, and with that type of formula in mind, it is no wonder that there were so many Jewish uprisings during the Roman Empire.

Back to the story. Haman did not make mention that it was the Jews who were a danger to the Persian Empire because Xerxes would have no reason to believe that the Jewish people were a threat at all. However, the mere mention of a threat to the kingdom at least convinced Xerxes to not stand in the way of Haman's ambition, at least not yet. Xerxes then gave his signet ring to Haman, which was interesting because by giving that ring to Haman, Xerxes was now giving Haman the responsibility to handle this supposed threat on his own. Ironically, even though Haman was now given king-like power, that power that he thought he had would end up sealing his fate.

Haman, however, was nothing if not devious and cunning. What did Haman do after having the king's approval of the removal of a "threat"? He designated a day, on the 13th day of the month of Adar on the Jewish calendar, to kill any and all Jews in the Persian Empire. "Wait a minute," you no doubt are wondering. "If Haman did not specifically say that the Jews were a threat to Xerxes's kingdom, how does he then state a day that the Jewish people must be killed, and have it be a law?" Simple, actually. Haman made this a law by stating that it was a decree that was made by Xerxes himself, not Haman, and by Xerxes giving Haman that signet ring, the letter was stamped by that ring, thus making the letter binding and approved by the king, and if you had a king who was supposed to be the supreme leader of the land, with nobody to put a check on his power, it was a law that could not be reversed unless the king did so himself. Although I am sure that Xerxes was not pleased with the methods that Haman was using, he could not, for the time being, reverse this law, because if he did, he might be perceived as a weak and indecisive king, or worse yet, as someone in a position of power who was untrustworthy.

Once Mordecai and most of the Jews found out about this plot devised by Haman, they were in great distress and mourning (and understandably so). This was a travesty, that anyone could make a law to allow an unwarranted genocide within the confines of his own kingdom. Mordecai, though, had an ace in the hole that Haman did not count on, and that was his cousin Esther. For many years, Mordecai had raised his cousin because she had no parents; now, it was Mordecai, and the Jewish people, for that matter, who needed Esther to step up to the plate and stop this plot from taking place. Esther found out about this plot from Mordecai, but she pointed out a sticking matter in all of this: in order to speak to the king, one must be called by him. Even the queen, which Esther was, had to follow this procedure. The lone exception was if the king were to extend his golden scepter to that person.

Once this was reported back to Mordecai, he pointed out what a Jew with sincere faith in God believed. Deliverance for the Jews would come, even if Esther were to refuse to help them. That was because the Jews were God's chosen people. He may have them dispersed to other nations, but He would never allow them to be completely wiped out in a genocide attempt. So, if Esther did not help, someone else would, but since Esther was in a position of responsibility, her refusal would mean that both her and her father's family would perish. Once Esther heard about the consequences of disobeying God, she told Mordecai to have all of the Jews in Susa fast and pray, and she would do likewise, as she decided to go to the king to speak with him, with or without his consent. If Esther was executed, she reasoned that at least it would be better than if she did nothing at all to help the people who raised her.

After three days of fasting, Esther went up to the king's entrance. Thankfully, as it turned out, the king was not only present but also pleased enough with Esther to extend his scepter to her. Xerxes asked what type of petition Esther wanted to make to him, to which she told him to come to a banquet that she was making and preparing, and also to bring Haman with him. The three had their dinner together, and again Xerxes asked what request Esther had in mind, and Esther said that she was willing to tell if Xerxes and Haman came to another banquet. Obviously, Esther was a bit scared, especially since what might have to happen was her revealing the race that she was a part of, and if she did that, she ran the risk of being killed by Haman, or perhaps even her own husband. In other words, you could say that Esther was working up her courage.

Once the meeting was over with for the evening, Haman was about as giddy as a school girl. Here he was, the second-in-command to the king, had vast wealth and many sons, and now, he and the king were the only ones invited to not one but two banquets hosted by the queen herself. Yet, there was also a sore spot. That Jew Mordecai, a man Haman felt deserved none of his respect, still refused to pay him homage, and this enraged Haman so much, in fact, that he was more focused on killing Mordecai and all the Jews than he was in all the successes that he had. Haman's wife, Zeresh, and all of his friends, suggested that Haman have a noose built 75 feet high and make a request to the king that Mordecai be hanged on it, and it was a plan that Haman was more than willing to go along with.

What is amazing in all of this was that not for one second did Haman think that maybe Esther might be

Jewish herself. If he had, he could have made the case that Esther was conspiring along with Mordecai to bring the Persian Empire down. Esther, however, with the help of Mordecai, was able to conceal her own identity, and it was this aspect that proved to be crucial in the saving of the Jewish people from seemingly certain destruction.

Another crucial thing that happened occurs the night before the second banquet that Esther was hosting for Xerxes and Haman. Apparently, Xerxes had some sort of nightmare; a nightmare that was so powerful and terrifying, in fact, that he could not sleep a wink, no matter how hard he tried. Truthfully, I think it was God's way of telling Xerxes that he was about to help in the execution of an innocent man; this, in spite of all that this man had done on behalf of Xerxes' kingdom. The reason why I think this is because how else do you explain that the first thing that Xerxes did once he woke up from one of his nightmares was have someone read to him about an event that happened years earlier? For it was while these chronicles on the reign of Xerxes were being read that someone stumbled upon the part where there was a plot to assassinate the king, but that it was uncovered by a man named Mordecai, the same one Haman had planned to kill, only Xerxes didn't know about it at the time. Xerxes then asked what type of favor was bestowed upon Mordecai for the uncovering of this plot, and as it turned out, nothing was done on his behalf. Not that Mordecai cared all that much about being honored; he only wanted to have a close relationship with God. However, it would have been nice if someone had done anything for him, since he had proven to be a loyal subject under the empire.

Xerxes, upon finding this out, wanted to honor Mordecai in some way. Now, on to possibly the most ironic part of this story. Just after Xerxes decided that he wants to honor Mordecai in some fashion, who should come but Haman, who had plans of his own, which was to tell the king to have Mordecai hung up on a noose. By this time, it was possible that maybe Xerxes suspected that there was something amiss about Haman, but he was not certain of it just yet. For the first thing Xerxes said to Haman was that he wanted to know how he was to go about honoring someone the king had found delight in. What Xerxes did not mention just yet was that he wanted to honor Mordecai, just as Haman did not initially make mention that it was the Jewish people he was accusing of rebelling against the Persian Empire.

By this time, Haman had grown accustomed to being honored, and definitely arrogant in his position of power, and he described in detail what he would like Xerxes to do for him, although he did not say as much. Furthermore, a noble prince in the kingdom should not only give this man a horse and a robe, but he should also parade the man being honored around the streets with the people giving this person the proper obedience that he deserved.

So what a shock it was to Haman's system when Xerxes asked him to do what he suggested for Mordecai. That had to stick in the craw of Haman, and he deserved to be humbled in some way, for him to parade around the very same man he had so much animosity towards that he wanted to have him hanged on a noose and kill everyone who belonged to the same race as Mordecai, but Haman did do this, much to his chagrin, because he knows two things: one, that even he could not disobey the king, and two, it only delayed somewhat his plot to kill Mordecai and the Jews.

Shortly afterwards was the big moment. Esther was going to make her request, and in this instance, she shined like never before. Esther was ready and prepared to make her case that both her and the Jews (although she only said that her people were being sold out for destruction; she still did not technically say that she was Jewish) should be spared from being slaughtered. Furthermore, Esther pointed out the most important truth: that it was Haman who was conspiring and plotting to wipe Esther's people off of the map. Xerxes was angry at Haman for this betrayal, and Haman made things even worse by petitioning before the queen but doing it in a way that appeared to Xerxes that Haman was about to harm Esther in some way. One of the eunuchs just so happened to have been on standby and pointed out to the king that Haman had made preparations in advance to have Mordecai, the one that Xerxes felt deserving of an honor, to be hung on a 75-foot noose. Xerxes decided to punish Haman by having him be strung up on that same noose instead, and later on, both Haman's wife and his sons were executed as well.

Esther and Mordecai were now safe, but it was not until Xerxes gave the Jews the right to defend themselves that a possible genocide was prevented. Instead of mourning and destruction, the day that Haman and his friends were supposed to utterly terminate the Jewish people turned into a day of celebration where the Jews once again were delivered from enemy hands. Later on, Mordecai was promoted to the very seat that Haman had before. Justice was done.

But what about Esther? Some said that she died after only five years as queen, while others contend that Xerxes sent her into exile, just as he had done with Vashti years earlier. Some even believe that Vashti eventually did return to her former post. Either situation is a possibility, given the poor medicine and sanitation of that era, as well as the temperament of Xerxes himself. The greatness of Esther, however, is not measured by her fate but by the fact that she was willing to lay it all down, even her life, in order to bring safety and peace to her own people, and that is why she should be measured as one of the great heroines in all of history.

Chapter 10
Daniel's Legacy
(The Book of Daniel)

Before Esther was around, there was a man who proved that while people are most often remembered by the big events of their lives, consistency in character is what prepares a person for the challenges ahead. I mean, what good is a person if he or she does not have the type of foundation in life that keeps him or her steady in both good times and in bad. Thus, this final chapter entails a man who might not have been called to build an ark like Noah or be the father of many nations like Abraham, was not given God's laws into some tablets like Moses or was not called to be an alpha dog kind a leader like Joshua or David, and while he could offer ofprophesy, was not the standard bearer of such ability as Elijah was, nor was he in a position to save his own people from genocide like Esther. However, this man still showed a consistency in serving God like the other characters in the Bible I have just now pointed out, and he still accomplished great things in his own right, this in spite of being thrown out of Jerusalem by a foreign army during his youth and living most of his life within the vast territory of his captors. I am talking about a man named Daniel.

At the start of Daniel's story, the kingdom of Judah was barely holding on by a thread. To be fair, the kingdom of Judah had some good kings, such as Hezekiah and Josiah (see 2 Kings 18–20; 22:1–23: 29). By the time Jehoiakim had begun to reign, however, the kingdom of Judah had sinned to the point where they could no longer distinguish between what was right and what was wrong. As a result, the nation had already by this time lost God's divine protection, which led to Babylon besieging Jerusalem. While the Babylonians did not completely destroy the city on that particular campaign, they made it perfectly clear that they were now the ones in control of the Judean kingdom. Later on, another king, this one by the name of Zedekiah, whom the Babylonians earlier had made the puppet king of Judah, made the foolish decision of trying to rebel against Babylon's orders and, for that matter, defied the message sent by another one of God's prophets, this one being Jeremiah (2 Kings 24:18–20 and Jeremiah 52), only to see Jerusalem destroyed.

However, it was during the first Babylonian invasion of Jerusalem that they rounded up, among others, Daniel and his friends Hananiah, Mishael, and Azariah, because the king of Babylon, most likely Nebuchadnezzer, was in need of young men who were not only physically fit but also intelligent as well, with a willingness to learn. Daniel's three friends were better known by their Babylonian names, with Hananiah being Shadrach, Mishael being Meshach, and Azariah being Abednego. Daniel himself was given the name Belteshazzar, but in this case, we will stick to calling him just plain Daniel.

For a mentor, Daniel and his friends were given a man by the name of Ashpenaz, who was a court official. It was his responsibility to teach these young men, among others, how to speak the Babylonian language and be able to read it as well. It was also his responsibility to make sure these men were well fed. But the dietary requirements that the Babylonians posted ran contradictory to the diet Daniel and some of the other Jews had, and it was Daniel who asked the court official permission not to defile himself with such foods. The court official was concerned about this and for good reason. He knew that if he consented to what Daniel had suggested to him, and if Daniel and his friends were to look worse for wear than those who were given food and its portions ascribed by Nebuchadnezzer himself, then that meant that this court official would lose his post and quite possibly be executed as well. Daniel did not necessarily have an argument over this issue, but he did suggest a compromise, and that was to see which ones looked better off after 10 days, those who followed the dietary restrictions of the king or those who ate as Daniel and his friends did.

Well, the 10 days came and went, and sure enough, it

was Daniel and his friends who looked to be the healthiest of the whole lot. The young Jewish men were then trained extensively on Babylonian culture for the next three years, and when the time came for the king to test them, it was Daniel, Shadrach, Meshach, and Abednego who stood above the rest; thus, they were allowed to serve under the king's court. Daniel at this point could already understand dreams and visions, a gift that would help him several times down the road.

One day, Nebuchadnezzer had a dream that disturbed him, and he needed someone who could interpret its meaning. Now, the Babylonians were a people interested in all sorts of mysterious arts, and by that I mean that they relied on magicians, enchanters, sorcerers, astrologers, and probably a few priests here and there, all in order to guide their leaders in things that might confound them. In other words, you are talking about a people that were extremely reliant on signs.

On this occasion, though, there was a curveball. You see, Nebuchadnezzer told all of these artists of dark magic about the fact that he had a dream, but he would not tell them what that dream was. Well, this proved to be an impossible problem to solve because in order to know the meaning of a dream, one has to know what that dream was in the first place. The problem here was that Nebuchadnezzer's servants were reliant on signs first, before being able to give its interpretation, and since they didn't even know what the signs were, that meant that they could not possibly interpret Nebuchadnezzer's dream.

Nebuchadnezzer, however, being paranoid like many rulers of nations are, believed that these men underneath him were merely using a delay tactic so that they could somehow overthrow him, even though what Nebuchadnezzer was asking was something that no man could possibly do. After all, it would take a god in order to figure out the interpretation of a dream but not have the exact details of that dream. In the meantime, Daniel and his friends had no clue as to what was going on, until Daniel asked Arioch, who was commander of the king's guards, about what was causing all this commotion. Upon finding out about the inability of the wise men of Babylon to interpret Nebuchadnezzer's dream, Daniel asked for more time before giving Nebuchadnezzer his answer.

One has to remember, though, that Daniel and his friends were also in danger, since they themselves were trained in learning about Babylonian culture from some of these exact wise men. Also, by Daniel asking for time, he was confirming what Nebuchadnezzer thought he already knew, which was that some of the wise men were plotting for his demise. The only saving grace was that Nebuchadnezzer had never specifically asked Daniel or his friends about what they thought of the dream, and since Daniel did not technically say no, the commander of the guards was at least willing to delay any execution.

What none of these wise men knew at the time, though, was that there was a god out there who could interpret dreams and be communicated to, who was the great I AM, as He had said many centuries earlier to Moses. According to Nebuchadnezzer's wise men, some of the ways of the "gods" were not supposed to be given to mortals, and interpretation of dreams but not being told by another mortal what those dreams were certainly was one of them. Daniel and his friends, however, grew up in a faith that believed that God answers prayers. All one has to do is simply ask Him, and you will surely have your answers at some point, which is what these four brave young men did. Lo and behold, Daniel has a vision of the same dream that Nebuchadnezzer had the night before, and now Daniel was ready to give the king of Babylon his answer.

So Daniel revealed the dream and its interpretation to Nebuchadnezzer, all the while pointing out that it was God alone who revealed such dreams to men; it was not by man's wisdom alone that such visions could be revealed and interpreted. The dream was as follows: Nebuchadnezzer saw this great statue, where the head was made of gold, its chest and arms were made out of silver, the stomach and thigh regions were made of bronze, the lower halves of the legs were made of iron, and its feet were part iron, part clay. While this statue looked impressive, a rock was cut out, but not by any man, and this rock crushed the feet of the statue, causing the rest of the pieces to be destroyed. No trace of the statue remained, but the rock that struck it turned into a great mountain.

Now, on to the interpretation of that same dream. Each part of the statue represented a nation or empire that would end up at some point being the most powerful on Earth. Since Babylon was the most powerful kingdom on Earth at the time, it represented the head, or gold. After that, another empire, supposedly inferior to Babylon's, would take over; thus, they represented the arms and chest, or silver. After that, a third kingdom came along, which would represent the bronze, followed up by a fourth kingdom that would crush all the others, as iron destroyed all other metals. After a time, a fifth kingdom appeared that was similar in some aspects to the kingdom that represented the iron portion of the statue's legs, but since its people were divided, it was represented as a combination of clay and iron, which did not stick together for long. Finally, the rock not cut out by human hands was an everlasting kingdom that would overthrow all the others.

While Daniel did not give the specific names of the kingdoms, since he did not know their specific identities, and since these were considered future kingdoms during Daniel's time, it can be safe to say which kingdoms represented what. The silver, for instance, represented the Medes and Persians, since their kingdom had rulers less powerful than Babylon's, and they came right after the Babylonians did. The bronze part of the statue represented Greece, as they would form the world's first democracy, and also since they started out united under Alexander the Great but then were divided into several different kingdoms after his death, which explained why the bronze started from the stomach, but then went down towards the upper part of the legs. The iron represented the Roman Empire, which as we mentioned in the previous chapter, was the first republic in the world, with its checks and balances between the executive and legislative branches, and did not infringe on the rights of the majority too much, with the exception being that of the Jewish people—that, and it was true that the Roman's did dominate any army that stood in its way. Also, the fact that this iron covered the lower half of both legs could mean that the Roman Empire was divided among themselves, both east and west.

Then you have the last two kingdoms, both of which were still to come, but one of which was being motioned by humans to make it such. The feet of the statue would represent a revived version of the Roman Empire, which explained the iron in it, but this empire would also have a mixture of peoples and nations that would have representation in it, although they did not get along with each other for very long, which was where the clay came into play. Also, since feet typically have 10 toes, those toes would represent the 10 kingdoms that would be controlled by this empire, and its leader would be the Antichrist revealed in Revelation 13–19. As we speak, the European nations are already getting closer to achieving this goal, first with the fact that they virtually have only one currency, the Euro, and second, the European Union has recently created a position of president, so things are starting to come in place for the Antichrist to take over the world for a short time.

God, however, will stop any more plans made by the Antichrist before he destroys all of humanity, and he will send his son Jesus Christ, who represents the rock that is not cut by human hands, and he will end the reign of the Antichrist and all those who serve him during the Great Tribulation. God's Kingdom, though, will be an everlasting kingdom, which is why the rock turns into a mountain, representing something that is unmovable.

Because of Daniel's ability to reveal this actual dream, as well as its interpretation, Nebuchadnezzer not only halted the execution of his wise men but also promoted Daniel into a higher position. Most shockingly, however, was that Nebuchadnezzer even acknowledged Daniel's God as being above all others. Even Daniel's friends, Meshach, Shadrach, and Abednego, were appointed as administrators over some of Babylon's provinces. As great as all of this was, however, Nebuchadnezzer lacked one characteristic that might have helped Babylon to delay its downfall, which was that he was anything but humble, as events would prove.

For what Nebuchadnezzer did next was build a statue made of gold that was 90 feet high, which would not have been the worst thing in the world, except that he demanded that all of the peoples within his kingdom bow down to it. In fact, anyone who refused to bow down to the image was to be thrown into a fiery furnace.

Of course, this was going to be a problem for Shadrach, Meshach, and Abednego, the very same friends of Daniel who were tested and questioned years earlier about their knowledge of Babylonian culture. You see, they worshipped the one true God and to bow down to this pagan idol went against anything and everything that they believed in, and so, they did what any God-fearing Jew would do and refused to bow down to Nebuchadnezzer's golden image.

Apparently, some of Nebuchadnezzer's astrologers took notice of this, which makes you wonder if they had some sort of inferiority complex or jealousy towards Daniel and his friends. So they mentioned the brave stand that Shadrach, Meshach, and Abednego took in regards to the golden image, except that Nebuchadnezzer was not going to think of this as a brave stand but rather as a rebellion against his kingdom. So Nebuchadnezzer had these three men summoned to him, and after making mention of their refusal to obey the king's order, decided to give them one last chance. The king figured that by giving Daniel's friends one last chance, he would seem to be merciful while still showing his absolute authority over his whole kingdom. If they did bow down, the king would forgo the execution, but if they still refused, then they surely would be thrown into the blazing furnace that he had designed, where these three men would be burnt alive.

There were two things to consider with this passage. One, Daniel was not present during this time. Maybe he had an errand to attend to, or he was busy governing one of Babylon's provinces. Who knows? In any event, the fact that Daniel was not present during this forced worship ceremony must have meant that there was no one to deter Nebuchadnezzer from his evil actions on that day.

Two, the other thing to consider, is that in the previous chapter, Nebuchadnezzer was praising Daniel and God Himself for having the ability to recognize his dream and interpret it as well. Now he was forcing Daniel's friends into denying the same God Daniel worshipped and making them bow down to this false idol that Nebuchadnezzer had made. Sometimes, it does make you wonder if Nebuchadnezzer was one of those who did believe that Daniel's God existed, but that he would only worship the great Jehovah Jireh for his own convenience, which is the same thing many people do on a regular basis. We tend to believe that God can and will provide for us, but we also have to worship Him on a daily basis and put our trust into His timing.

Anyway, Shadrach, Meshach, and Abednego brave-ly stuck to their guns, and when given this second opportunity, still would not worship this pagan image that Nebuchadnezzer had made. What was especially remarkable was that these three men were even willing to risk their lives for it. Yes, they had full confidence that God could get them out of this predicament alive and unscathed, but even if they were to lose their lives, it was better if they did so while still trusting in their Lord, instead of compromising their values and losing their very souls in the process.

Yes, this stance that Daniel's friends took was very courageous, but it did not change the fact that Nebuchadnezzer was now even more irate at these men than he was before. In fact, Babylon's king was so displeased that he not only had Shadrach, Meshach, and Abednego thrown into the fiery furnace but he also had it heated up seven times as much as before. Also, some of the strongest men in Babylon tied these men up with very strong ropes, to ensure that there would be no escape. It seemed like Daniel's buddies would suffer a martyr's death.

To tell you how impossible it should have been for Shadrach, Meshach, and Abednego to survive such a tough ordeal, the men who threw those three into that furnace fell in themselves and perished. If those who were not tied up died from the heat of the furnace, there should have been no way for the three Jewish men who refused to worship the golden idol, who were tied up by some of the strongest men in all of Babylon, to have lived to tell the tale. Yet, when Nebuchadnezzer went to look again, he saw something very strange. Apparently, Shadrach, Meshach, and Abednego were now just standing there unbound and unchained, as if they were in the comforts of their own homes, and also, there was a fourth man there, as well, talking with them. This fourth man, however, looked more like the son of God than any ordinary individual. At this, Nebuchadnezzer could not believe what he had just witnessed, but instead of completely losing his cool over the God of Abraham, Issac, and Jacob proving to be superior to him or his gods, Nebuchadnezzer was almost overjoyed that no harm had come to these Jewish men, and he was never so proud to be proven wrong; thus, he called them out to see if they were alive, which they were. When it came time to get these men out of the furnace, it turned out that the flames had such little effect on Shadrach, Meshach, and Abednego that not even the stench of smoke could be found on them, which is even more remarkable, because any stove that a person could come across, if they stood nearby, would leave the smell of smoke on them for quite some time, even if they never got burnt.

In the meantime, however, Daniel's services, and his

ability to interpret dreams, were needed. In this next dream that Nebuchadnezzer had, there was a magnificent tree that all sorts of plant life and animals lived under, and this tree even provided food for every creature. In fact, the tree was so enormous that it could even touch the sky. However, a holy one sent by heaven had a message, a message that came to pass, that the tree should be cut down, its branches trimmed, but the root of it, and its stump, should be preserved while bound by iron and bronze. Afterwards, the tree was forced to live among the animals with the dew of heaven and was in this animalistic state until seven times pass by him.

When Daniel was summoned to interpret this dream, he did not want to tell the king at first because he knew it was something bad for Nebuchadnezzer, and if the king of Babylon did not like what he heard, there was ample reason to believe that he would kill Daniel. What the dream meant was that Nebuchadnezzer was the tree, and as such, his kingdom had become great in the eyes of men, to the point where his influence could be felt all over the known world. However, since he had failed to acknowledge the God who makes kings and gives them power, Nebuchadnezzer would be stripped of his power. For a time, he would live worse than a commoner, not even having any shelter, and thus, he would wind up living like an animal. Seven times could be any given time period, but the fact that the stump and root of the tree was preserved with iron and bronze meant that Nebuchadnezzer had the opportunity to be restored to power once he realized that it is God alone who rules the world. Needless to say, everything that Daniel interpreted came to pass, and for a while, Nebuchadnezzer did live even worse than a slave once he was thrown out of his kingdom.

Eventually, however, Nebuchadnezzer did turn from his proud ways, and he became a great king. Unfortunately, this turnaround through the humbling of oneself and acknowledgement of God was lost on many of the Babylonians. At some point after the death of Nebuchadnezzer, the fate of his successor, Belshazzar, would already be written on the wall— quite literally, in fact. Somehow, the golden goblets that the Babylonians had confiscated when they besieged and destroyed Jerusalem many years before were now being drunk by Belshazzar and his nobles. Instead of praising God, however, like Nebuchadnezzer did once he humbled himself, the people of Babylon were now praising their false idols, ones that were made by their own hands.

All of a sudden, however, a hand that looked like that of a human's began writing a message on some plaster that was being used for a wall. This obviously terrified everybody in attendance, to the point where I am sure they didn't have any rational thought left, but nobody could interpret or read the message, not even Belshazzar himself, nor the wise men. Belshazzar's wife, however, knew of someone who could read and interpret the message, someone who had done such things previously for Nebuchadnezzer but who seemed to have been all but forgotten by this particular king.

So, at the request of the new king, Belshazzar, Daniel was once again summoned for his abilities as an interpreter, only this time it was to read a simple message and not to tell the meaning of a dream. Daniel did read the message, then pointed out that because Belshazzar had not humbled himself, as Nebcuhadnezzer had during his exile, yet Belshazzar knew of Nebuchadnezzer's story, the message was sent that said, "Mene, mene, Tekel, Parsin." "Mene" was God numbering the days of Belshazzar's reign, and brought it to an end. "Tekel" was God weighing the scales, which showed in Belshazzar that he lacked humbleness and a willingness to acknowledge God. "Parsin" meant that the time of the Babylonians was ending and would be taken over by the Medes and Persians.

Belshazzar was just happy that someone interpreted the writing on the wall. Thus, he basically treated Daniel like royalty, even going so far as to declare Daniel third in line to the throne. Which I am sure that Daniel did appreciate. However, I think Daniel would have been happier if Belshazzar had fully understood the meaning of this message, instead of just giving Daniel a more prominent role in the Babylonian kingdom. The biggest problem was that even in this instance, Belshazzar didn't do the one thing that might have averted such disaster from happening to both him and his kingdom, and that was to praise God for showing him this sign. Instead, Belshazzar believed that Daniel basically was able to interpret the writing on the wall by himself, without any divine help. Another thing Belshazzar did not comprehend, until it was too late, was that on this very night, he was to be killed, and a man named Darius was to take over as king. It was Darius, as events would unfold, who was to be ruler and play a role in the most famous part in Daniel's life.

Now, one of the first deeds of Darius was to appoint 120 satraps, whom one could have said to be representatives, or possibly advisors, to rule over the kingdom. However, three administrators were also appointed, probably, to keep the satraps accountable to how the government was run, with one of the administrators, as it turned out, being Daniel. Of course, just as he had in his youth, Daniel had to be exceptional in his work, so much so, in fact, that Darius planned to give Daniel a role in overseeing the entire kingdom. Basically, one could say that this was a role similar to that of Joseph in the book of Genesis, where he was second-in-command to Pharaoh himself. Needless to say, the other administrators and satraps were immensely jealous, and possibly even a little threatened, by Daniel's possible promotion, so they conspired to see what charges they could bring against him.

At first, they were to be disappointed. Daniel had

integrity, and because of that integrity, he could not be corrupted nor be accused of neglecting or perverting his duty to handle justice. These conspirators, however, were nothing if not persistent, figuring that if they could find no evidence of Daniel being corrupt and lacking integrity on an existing law, that meant that they had to create some sort of new law, but what could it be? Eventually, they came to the realization that they could not attack Daniel's character, which was nothing but outstanding, but maybe they could find something that Daniel believed in and use it against him.

So, the government officials came up with a strategy. They made a request to the king, which stated that everybody who was either part of the government or an advisor agreed that anybody who was caught worshipping or praying to a man or a god who was not a king be put inside a lion's den, and, in fact, had the king state it and put it in writing, so that this law would be binding. What they did not say is that nobody talked to Daniel about this law, and there were two good reasons for this. One, they wanted desperately to eliminate Daniel from office, and two, even if that was not their intent, which it was, the officials under Darius knew that Daniel would never have gone with such a law, so it was best to have Daniel kept in the dark about something like this. One had to remember that these men probably had heard of the story many years beforehand of how Daniel's friends disobeyed

Nebuchadnezzer's command to bow down to a golden image, even to the point of death. After all, if Daniel's friends showed that much dedication to their God, and since Daniel did worship that same God, there was no reason to believe that Daniel would not show that type of devotion to the deity he worshipped.

Darius, of course, was thinking with his ego, because after all, what man of that era would not want people to bow down before him? He even agreed with the length that this particular law was to be implemented, which was 30 days. Like I said before, it was only natural for a human being to want to be treated with some sort of respect, and there was no greater respect that could be given to a person than if he or she were treated like a god. Certainly, that temptation would have to be there, especially for someone who was in the position of power that Darius was in.

Daniel, upon finding out about news concerning this new law, must have been distraught and terrified for his life. What was great, though, was that Daniel's response to such adversity was what made Daniel one of the all-time great characters in biblical history. He could have followed those orders, stating how great Darius was, all in hopes of not only saving his own life but also maintaining the position that Darius had just now entrusted him to. Honestly, in such circumstances, would anyone have blamed Daniel for following the status quo, especially if everybody else was going to? Well, as it turned out, Daniel did, in fact, stick to his principles, where he would continue praising God three times a day, with his window open, just as he had always done beforehand.

Does this mean that we should pray to God exactly three times each and every day? Of course not! However, what the story of Daniel tells us in this instance is that we should be consistent in serving the Lord throughout our lives, even in the face of persecution, and even if everyone else might think that serving God is lame and uncool and not within line of current trends. In this instance, Daniel passed that particular test with flying colors.

That being said, what we see as taking a stand for biblical principles, back then, the other officials, who wanted Daniel removed from his position, saw as the opportunity that they had been looking for. It was obvious that Daniel was still serving his God instead of worshipping the king of Babylon. And since this law was binding, and it appeared to be irreversible, Daniel was now to be taken to the lion's den and thrown into it.

Oh, Darius did not want to do such a thing. After all, Daniel had proven to be the most effective and trustworthy administrator in all the land. Daniel had, in fact, always been known as a man of integrity. However, Darius also knew the edict he made, one that was now law in accordance with the Medes and Persians, and to explain why a king of Babylon would have laws based in accordance with Medes and Persians, it must be pointed out that Darius was one of two things. He was a puppet leader used by the Medes and Persians to overthrow the Babylonians, just as the Babylonians had basically done to the kingdom of Judah, or it was possible, and there are those who believe this, that Darius might have been the ruler of Persia himself, Cyrus, the very same one who made an edict early into his reign that the Jewish people were allowed to return to their homeland and start the rebuilding of Jerusalem.

In any event, this also showed the difference between the way the Babylonians governed their own people and the way the Medes and Persians did. For the Babylonians, while they did have one king who was supreme over everyone else, whose authority was to be left unquestioned, were at least allowed to change their laws as they saw fit, whereas in the Persian Empire, while the king at that time was at least allowing some input among his officials and cabinet, once he made a law binding according to Mede and Persian customs, that law could almost never be changed, even by the king who created such a law in the first place. If nothing else, the Persians did value the spoken word.

So Daniel was indeed thrown into the lion's den. That should have been the be all and end all. Daniel should have surely been torn into tiny pieces by those lions. Even a stone was put in place so that there was no way that he could have possibly escaped. Later on that night, Darius could not sleep because he kept thinking to himself that he might have sent an innocent man to be executed in such a gruesome manner, and who could blame the man for thinking so?

Only thing was, something big did occur, as Darius found out the following day. Daniel's God had actually protected him in that lion's den, because an angel appeared out of nowhere and shut the mouths of those dreadful lions. Remember, the den was covered by a stone for the purpose of preventing both aid to the person condemned to die and escape, and I am sure that such a stone was designed to be extremely heavy and impossible for any one person to move by himself or herself. Also, even if the stone didn't weigh something like a metric ton, the fact that Darius had a lock on it should have made it so. Under such circumstances, there was no way any man could have possibly been prevented from turning into some sort of lion's hamburger meat. Yet, Daniel somehow not only survived but did so without even a scratch upon him.

Once Darius found out about this, he not only had Daniel pulled out of the den but sent Daniel's accusers and their families into that same den that Daniel had been put in earlier for their treachery. Sure enough, the lions wound up gobbling and destroying those people before they even had touch the ground. Yes, Daniel's faith in God had preserved him yet again, and his enemies got their just desserts, as I am certain that those lions enjoyed human flesh quite a bit.

Just like with other kings whom he served, Daniel prospered greatly under the reign of Darius. However, Daniel's impact could not have been felt with just how he had served under kings from a foreign nation. If he were merely just another advisor, nobody would be hearing about his stories some 2,500 years later. The last six chapters in the book of Daniel deal with visions and prophecies that God had bestowed upon His loyal servant. Some, such as the transferring of kingdoms in chapters 7 and 8 have already taken place, for the most part, while others are events that have yet to occur. What is even more interesting was that many of these prophecies can also be found in the book of Revelation.

In the end, though, what can we learn about Daniel and, for that matter, other characters in the Bible like him? It is not those who are the strongest, or the bravest, or even the most intelligent who achieve greatness in the eyes of our Lord. God is not impressed by those who have great riches or great power, although He most certainly can provide those things to those who ask of Him. No, the true mark of greatness is measured by those who make the King of kings and Lord of lords the top priority in their lives. It is measured not by the bragging of what one has but rather by random acts of kindness, some of which do not even cross our minds, and for no personal gain. Finally, greatness is measured by those who are willing to serve, and to serve others is far more important than whether or not we have others bend down and serve our needs. It is such selflessness that is required to be called children of God, like Daniel and others who obey God's word already are.

Conclusion

"Wait a minute." Some of you are doubting. "You mean to tell me that this book only covers somewhere around 200 pages, and that all there is to this book are a bunch of reenactments of the Old Testament? Where is the intrigue and how any of this stuff applies to my daily life?" Ah, but you see, such foolish thinking means that you are not reading between the lines. There is a lot more to this than meets the eye.

In chapter 1, for instance, what we uncovered are the origins of our planet, plus where earthly death originated from. Those who say that it is unfair for a good person to die usually do not realize that death would not have existed had man and woman both obeyed God's command not to eat of the Tree of Knowledge, knowing good and evil. Also, just because a person dies does not automatically mean that life was in vain. For many, in fact, it is a legacy where they contribute something to future generations that makes them so memorable. Each and every story in the Bible, one could say, is the result of people leaving a legacy on Earth, whether it be good or bad.

Another thing to consider is this: you have a bunch of

people in the stories that I have mentioned who stood by on their principles and belief in God, no matter how dire the circumstances, and I am only scratching the surface on this one. Noah still built the ark that saved him, his family, and all the animals he was commanded by God to save, all of this, in spite of the fact that he had never even built a boat, and everyone else in the entire world was ridiculing him. In chapter 3, you had Abraham having the courage of leaving the comfortable surroundings of the town of Ur, to go into a land that he did not know anything about, with the promise that it was to be on that land that he was to be the father of many nations, in spite of the fact that his wife Sarah was barren until the age of 90. Also that chapter explained why homosexuality is considered a sin and an abomination and why those who support such a lifestyle are in opposition to God's will and not in alignment with it.

You have Moses, who should not even have survived a childhood that was ruled by an oppressive Pharaoh who wanted the slaughter of every male child in Egypt, who went into hiding once he killed an Egyptian slave master, only to come back onto that very land 40 years later, forced Pharaoh's hand (with help from God, of course) into freeing the Hebrew slaves, and led them through 40 years of wasteland, while still seeing God make the 10 Commandments firsthand, not once but twice.

Let us not forget about leaders such as Joshua, who

had the pressure of living up to Moses's shoes, and who still found a way to trust in the Lord as he won victory after victory, nor should we forget about Samuel, who, as the last judge of Israel, still served the Lord diligently, even while those who were respected in the Israelite community, such as Eli and Saul, proved to be corrupted and blinded the eyes of justice. David, who was another fine example of someone the Lord used in spite of being only a child, grew up to be a great king, not because he bragged about himself in the third person all the time but because he was willing to humble himself when he did wrong, and gave credit to God when victory was achieved. All it took for David was five stones and a sling, and look at what he accomplished later on.

Then you had Elijah, who still was proclaiming God's word and message, even when leaders of his own people in Israel were worshipping a pagan god and threatening his life. Elijah proved in his story time and time again that just because those in a position of power refused to serve the Lord, that did not mean that they could intimidate you if you only stood on His promises. Yes, there were trials where Elijah needed the Lord to strengthen him, because of how hard the journey was, but isn't that what the Lord wants us to do, anyway, to rely on Him, instead of our own wisdom and understanding, even in the midst of the tough times?

Also, how could we forget about Esther, who was a

definite role model for women in this day in age? Here was a lady who lived in a male-dominated society that would even scoff at the thought of a lady being able to read and write, yet it was she who had the courage and foresight to save her fellow Jews from a genocide plot made by a madman who wanted revenge for what had happened 500 years before. Anybody who was willing to sacrifice his or her own life and break the customs of the empire that he or she was serving under deserves some sort of praise.

Finally, what about Daniel? This was a man who early in his childhood was taken away from his homeland through force. He could have been bitter at those who not only captured him and his friends but also besieged and destroyed his beloved city of Jerusalem. It would have even been understandable if he had wanted some sort of revenge on the Babylonians and committed any sort of atrocity in order to do so. However, what Daniel did was make the best out of a situation that he did not want to be in, and he became a loyal servant in Babylon, while at the same time telling those leaders in that kingdom where they went wrong and also maintaining his principles and willingness to worship only God Himself. It is also encouraging to know that Daniel's friends Shadrach, Meshach, and Abednego all shared in this same belief.

That being said, if you think that these are the only characters in the Bible or even, for that matter, the Old

Testament, from whom somebody could get a good lesson or have passages interpreted for them, you are sadly mistaken. Like I said before, these stories only cover the surface of what can be explained if you just took the time to read the Bible and pray. It is just the tip of the iceberg, and I am most certainly willing to write more (for dramatic effect) <u>Stories of the Old Testament</u>, as well as write some about Jesus and the New Testament, in the near future.

Bibliography

Books
Revolution
Copyright 2000 by Michael Brown pg. 260
Published by Regal Books.

All Bible Verses came from:
The NIV Study Bible: 10th Anniversary Edition
Copyright 1995 by Zondervan

The Bible as History
Copyright 1956 by Werner Keller

Videos

Moses: Man of God
Copyright 2005
Grizzly Adams Family Entertainment

Biblical Old Testament Mysteries
Copyright 2005
Grizzly Adams Family Entertainment

CPSIA information can be obtained
at www.ICGtesting.com
Printed in the USA
FFOW02n1122130616
24964FF